The Return of The Great Brain

OTHER YEARLING BOOKS YOU WILL ENJOY:

The Great Brain, JOHN D. FITZGERALD

More Adventures of the Great Brain, JOHN D. FITZGERALD

Me and My Little Brain, JOHN D. FITZGERALD

The Great Brain at the Academy, JOHN D. FITZGERALD

The Great Brain Reforms, JOHN D. FITZGERALD

Henry Reed, Inc., KEITH ROBERTSON

Henry Reed's Journey, KEITH ROBERTSON

Henry Reed's Baby-Sitting Service, KEITH ROBERTSON

How to Eat Fried Worms, THOMAS ROCKWELL

The Clay Pot Boy, CYNTHIA JAMESON

YEARLING BOOKS are designed especially to entertain and enlighten young people. The finest available books for children have been selected under the direction of Charles F. Reasoner, Professor of Elementary Education, New York University.

For a complete listing of all Yearling titles,
write to Education Sales Department, Dell Publishing Co., Inc.,
1 Dag Hammarskjold Plaza, New York, N.Y. 10017

The Return of The Great Brain

ILLUSTRATED BY MERCER MAYER

by John D. Fitzgerald

A YEARLING BOOK

Published by
Dell Publishing Co., Inc.
1 Dag Hammarskjold Plaza
New York, New York 10017

Yearling ® TM 913705, Dell Publishing Co., Inc.
ISBN: 0-440-45941-9
Reprinted by arrangement with The Dial Press
Printed in the United States of America
Ninth Dell printing—October 1981
CW

For Phyllis and Jean

Contents

The Return of The Great Brain

CHAPTER ONE

The Adenville Academy

DURING THE FIRST WEEK of August in the year 1898 a trial was held in Adenville, Utah. The defendant was my brother, Tom Fitzgerald, alias The Great Brain. He was only twelve years old, but he was charged with being a confidence man, a swindler, a crook, and a blackmailer. The judge was Harold Vickers, who was sixteen. And I guess I must have been the youngest district attorney to ever try a case, because I was only ten years old.

I hated to put my brother on trial, but it was something the kids in Adenville should have done a long time before we did. Tom, with his great brain and his money-loving heart had been swindling us kids since he was eight years old. We had put up with it until that summer. He had swindled Danny Forester out of his new baseball glove, Parley Benson out of his new King air rifle, and a dozen other kids including myself. But when Tom almost got my two best friends killed to make thirty cents, I decided the only way to make him give up his crooked ways was to put him on trial in our barn.

If I do say so myself I presented a brilliant case, calling one witness after another to testify The Great Brain had swindled them. I wanted to take the witness stand myself because Tom had swindled and blackmailed me more than any kid in town. But Judge Harold Vickers said I couldn't be both a witness and the district attorney.

Tom was found guilty on all counts. Harold handed down the sentence: No kid in Adenville would play with The Great Brain or have anything to do with him for one year. After Tom promised to reform, Harold suspended the sentence. But he warned Tom that if my brother did any backsliding he would revoke the suspended sentence.

There was great rejoicing all over town when the results of the trial became known. Papa, who was editor and publisher of the *Adenville Weekly Advocate*, was so happy he looked ten years younger. I guess that was because Tom's past shenanigans had made him look ten years older. Now he wouldn't have to worry about angry fathers coming into his office to complain that Tom had cheated their sons out of something.

Mamma was happy as a bee in its first spring flower. Mothers of the boys my brother had swindled would no longer be calling her on the telephone to tell her she had a junior-grade confidence man for a son. My uncle, Mark Trainor, who was the town marshal and a deputy sheriff, was relieved because he would no longer have to explain why he couldn't put Tom in jail. Tom, with his great brain, had been so smart there never was enough evidence to arrest him.

The way people acted it was a wonder Mayor Calvin Whitlock didn't declare a holiday to celebrate The Great Brain's reformation. But for my money everybody was living in a temporary fool's paradise. I didn't believe The Great Brain could give up his crooked ways any more than a hen with a rooster around could stop laying eggs. But after a whole week went by without Tom pulling one crooked stunt I began to think maybe he really was going to reform. And strangely enough I began to regret it. I had never realized how dull things would be if Tom reformed. His crooked deals and swindles made life exciting even when I was the victim.

I was thinking about this one morning as I sat on the log railing of our corral fence with Tom and our six-year-old adopted brother, Frankie. Frankie's parents and brother had been killed in a landslide when he was four. When Uncle Mark couldn't locate any other relatives, Mamma and Papa had adopted him. It was easy to see that Frankie wasn't our real brother because he had the blackest, straightest hair of any kid in town. I was a dead ringer for Papa with dark eyes and dark curly hair. My oldest brother, Sweyn, who was named after our maternal Danish grandfather, had blond hair like Mamma. Tom didn't look like Mamma and Papa unless you sort of put them together. He was the only one in the family with freckles.

So there I was sitting on the corral fence that morning wondering if I'd made a mistake putting Tom on trial and making him reform.

"Going swimming this afternoon?" I asked.

"Sure, J.D.," Tom answered. "What made you ask such a silly question?"

My brothers and I often called each other by our initials because that was the way Papa usually addressed us. We all had the same middle name of Dennis just like Papa because it was a tradition in our family.

"I just wanted to see if they've started to grow yet," I said.

"What are you talking about?" Tom asked.

"Yeah, what?" Frankie said.

"You've been such a good little angel since you reformed," I said, "all you need are some wings."

"You were the one who got the kids to put me on trial and make me promise to reform," Tom said. "Are you sorry I have reformed?"

"You've become so goody-goody it makes me sick," I said. "There is no fun and excitement any more."

"So," Tom said, "you want fun and excitement. In other words, J.D., you are trying to make a backslider out of me."

Frankie looked up at Tom. "What's a backslider?" he asked.

"A backslider," Tom said, "is a person who promises to reform and then doesn't keep his promise. But do you know what is ten times worse than a backslider? I'll tell you. It is a person who tries to get somebody who has promised to reform to backslide. And I'm afraid when I tell Papa and Mamma about it that J.D. is going to find himself in hot water."

"I'm not trying to make a backslider out of you," I protested.

"Oh, yes, you are," Tom said. "And Frankie is my witness."

Frankie patted Tom on the knee. "Tom is good now," he said, "and you are trying to make him bad again."

"How right you are, Frankie," Tom said as he jumped down from the corral fence. "I think we should let Mamma and Papa know about this right away."

I jumped down from the fence. I knew it would cost me at least a month's allowance if they told.

"How much do you want not to tell?" I asked.

"That proves it," Tom said. "If I ask you for anything to make me keep silent that would be blackmail. You want to make a blackmailer out of me just so you can make a backslider out of me."

"No, I don't," I protested. "I'm sorry I opened my big mouth."

"Just being sorry isn't enough," Tom said. "You must be punished for trying to make a backslider out of me."

I knew he had me. "Name the punishment," I said.

"No," Tom said. "You must punish yourself."

"How can I punish myself?" I asked.

Tom looked up at Frankie who was still sitting on the fence. "Know something, Frankie?" he said. "Mamma wants the vegetable garden weeded tomorrow. One way J.D. could punish himself would be to volunteer to weed the garden all by himself."

It was a stiff price to pay for not having sense enough to keep my big mouth shut. It would take me all day to weed the garden without Tom's help. Mamma wouldn't let Frankie help with the weeding because he didn't know the difference between a weed and a vegetable.

"I'll punish myself," I said. "I'll weed the garden."

"All right," Tom said. "And to show you my heart is in the right place, I'll do your share of the chores tomorrow."

He boosted Frankie down from the fence. "Let's go to Smith's lot and play until lunch time," he said.

Mr. Smith let the kids use a vacant lot he owned on Main Street in return for keeping it cleared of weeds. Main Street was a very wide street like in most Utah towns. It was covered with a foot of gravel so it wouldn't get muddy when it rained. There were electric light and telephone poles down the middle of the street, and the sides were lined with trees planted by early Mormon pioneers. The places of business all had wooden sidewalks and hitching posts in front of them. The railroad tracks separated the east side of town from the west side. Most of the places of business and practically all the homes were on the west side, including the *Advocate* office and our home. East of the railroad tracks there were two saloons, the Sheepmen's Hotel, the Palace Cafe, a rooming house, a livery stable, and the campgrounds.

Adenville was an agricultural community surrounded by farms and cattle and sheep ranches. It never got very cold in the wintertime, and we seldom had snow because the town was located in southwestern Utah. We had a population of about two thousand Mormons, four hundred Protestants, and only about a hundred of us Catholics. The Mormons had a tabernacle and a Bishop because Adenville was what the Church of Jesus Christ of Latter-day Saints called a ward. There was no Protestant or Catholic church. We all went to the Community Church where Reverend Holcomb preached strictly from the Bible so he wouldn't show favoritism toward any religion.

As Tom, Frankie, and I walked down Main Street toward Smith's vacant lot I couldn't help feeling relieved that Adenville had only a one-room schoolhouse, where Mr. Standish taught the first through the sixth grades. Any parents wanting their kids to get a higher education had to send them to Provo or Salt Lake City. In just two weeks Tom would be leaving for his second year at the Catholic Academy for Boys in Salt Lake City. He would be in the eighth grade this year although he was only twelve. Tom with his great brain had been so smart that Mr. Standish had let him skip the fifth grade. My brother Sweyn had already graduated from the Academy, where only the seventh and eighth grades were taught. Papa was sending Sweyn to live with relatives in Boylestown, Pennsylvania, where he would go to high school.

If I could just keep my big mouth shut for two weeks I wouldn't have to worry about Tom making me the victim of his great brain and money-loving heart. I knew he hadn't really reformed when he blackmailed me into weeding the garden. I also knew it would break Mamma's and Papa's hearts if they found out Tom was backsliding. And I had a feeling that Tom wasn't worried about the suspended sentence. He would be going away for nine months and probably figured the kids would forget all about the trial by the following summer.

When we arrived at the lot there were about twenty kids playing catch, batting fly balls, playing leapfrog, broad jumping, and playing other games. We joined in until it was time to go home for lunch.

That evening after the supper dishes were washed and put away the whole family was sitting in the parlor. Aunt Bertha was sitting on the couch darning socks. She wasn't really our aunt. She had come to live with us after her husband died because she didn't have any place to go. She was in her sixties, with hands and feet as big as a man's. Mamma was sitting in her maple rocking chair knitting. Frankie, Tom, and I were sitting on the floor in front of the stone fireplace playing dominoes. Sweyn was reading a book. Mamma looked up from her knitting with a sort of sad expression on her face.

"I was just thinking, dear," she said to Papa, "with two of our boys going away to school soon we haven't many more evenings to spend together as a family."

"That reminds me," Papa said. "Everything is arranged for Sweyn to go back east. But next week I must remember to send Father Rodriguez a check for two hundred and twenty-five dollars to enroll Tom for the school year at the Catholic Academy."

"I wish we had an academy right here in Adenville," Mamma said.

"Few if any towns this size in Utah have more than a common school with six grades," Papa said. "There just aren't enough parents who want their children to get more than a sixth grade education, especially in an agricultural community like Adenville. Many farmers believe you don't need more than a sixth grade education to run a farm. Take Adenville—not more than a dozen boys and girls are sent to academies or high schools each year."

"I think a lot of parents would like their children to get a higher education, but they just can't afford it," Mamma said.

"Two hundred to two hundred and fifty dollars for a school year is a lot of money," Papa said. "That is what the

Mormon, Protestant, and Catholic boarding school academies charge."

"It just isn't fair for a boy like Sammy Leeds," Mamma said. "He has been working now for over a year on the soda fountain at the drugstore. Mr. Nicholson told me the boy wants to become a pharmacist more than anything in this world. But he hasn't got a chance because Mr. and Mrs. Leeds can't afford to send him to an academy."

Papa appeared puzzled. "It takes more than an eighth grade education to become a pharmacist," he said.

"I know," Mamma said. "But Mr. Nicholson said that if Sammy had an eighth grade education he could get the boy a job working part time in a drugstore in Provo. By working there part time during the school year and full time here in Adenville during summer vacation, Sammy would be able to put himself through high school. Then Mr. Nicholson would help him prepare for the junior pharmacist state board examination. Instead Sammy Leeds will never be anything better than a soda fountain clerk."

"I see what you mean," Papa said. "By the time the boy saved enough money working for Mr. Nicholson to go to an academy, he would be so old that he would be ashamed to go. It would take him several years."

"The Leeds boy isn't the only one in this town to suffer," Mamma said. "I was talking to Mrs. Smith at the Ladies Sewing Circle meeting last week. I mentioned Sweyn D. and Tom D. would be leaving for school soon. She said that she and her husband had tried every way they could to send their son Seth to an academy but just couldn't make it."

"So that is why he tried to sell that vacant lot where the

kids play," Papa said. "He put an ad in the *Advocate* but told me the best offer he received was a hundred and twenty-five dollars."

"It meant so much to them," Mamma said, "because Mr. Wilson told them he would hire Seth as a clerk in his hay, grain, and feed store if he got an eighth grade education. Instead the boy will no doubt end up working at some menial job like his father. It just isn't fair."

"I wonder," Papa said, "how many boys and girls there are in town like Sammy Leeds and Seth Smith who are being deprived of making something of themselves because we don't have an academy here in Adenville." Then he leaned forward in his chair and spoke to Tom. "T.D.," he said, "how many boys do you know like Sammy and Seth who would like to get a higher education but whose parents can't afford it?"

Tom looked up from the domino game which he was winning easily. "A few," he said. "For one, Parley Benson. He wants to become a veterinary. He's always hanging around old Doc Stone and bringing the vet any animals he finds who need help. Doc Stone said that if Parley went through the eighth grade he'd take him on as an apprentice and make a veterinary out of him. But Parley told me his folks can't afford to send him away to school. I guess he'll end up a bounty hunter like his father, and that is going to be tough on him because he loves all animals."

Papa leaned back in his rocking chair. "You and your mother have given me an idea," he said. "The way things are, parents who can afford it send their children away to Mormon, Protestant, and Catholic boarding school academies. But if we had a nondenominational academy right here in Adenville they would enroll their children in it. And there must be quite a few people like the parents of Seth Smith, Sammy Leeds, and Parley Benson who can't afford to send their children away to school but who could afford a tuition of thirty or forty dollars at an academy here in town. Add these students to the dozen or so who would otherwise be sent away to school and the tuition money would pay for a teacher."

Mamma shook her head. "That still leaves an academy to be built," she said.

Did that stop Papa? Heck no. He had an answer for everything.

"I'm sure, Tena," he said, "there are enough public-spirited citizens who would donate the money, material, and labor to build an academy if they knew for certain we could enroll about thirty students. I'll see Mayor Whitlock first thing in the morning and then talk to Bishop Aden and the Reverend Holcomb. This will have to be a united effort of Mormons, Protestants, and Catholics."

The next morning during breakfast Mamma reminded Tom and me that she wanted the vegetable garden weeded.

"I'm going to weed the garden myself," I said, "and Tom is going to do my share of the chores."

Papa stared at me as if I had a cabbage for a head and then looked with suspicion at Tom.

"Just how did you connive your brother into weeding the garden in exchange for doing his share of the chores?" he demanded. "If I catch you backsliding you are going to regret it."

"Who is backsliding?" Tom asked looking as innocent as a little baby. "J.D. told me yesterday that he wanted to weed the garden to punish himself. Out of the goodness of my heart I told him that I would do his share of the chores."

"Punish himself for what?" Papa asked.

I was afraid Tom would tell and get me into more trouble than himself. "I did something that I shouldn't have done," I said. "I'm so ashamed that I want to punish myself for doing it."

Mamma looked at Papa. "Maybe he broke a neighbor's window playing ball or something," she said.

"No, I didn't," I said.

"Then what did you do?" Mamma asked.

"I can't tell you because it's personal," I said.

Papa saved me. "Let's respect the boy's privacy," he said, "as long as we know he wasn't forced into weeding the garden by T.D."

Boy, oh, boy, that brother of mine was something. He looked Papa right in the eye.

"You don't have to say it, Papa," Tom said. "I know you are sorry you accused me of backsliding, and I accept your apology."

I began weeding the garden after breakfast while Tom and Frankie did the chores. When they finished, Tom saddled up Sweyn's mustang, Dusty, and went for a ride. Eddie Huddle came over to play with Frankie. They started pitching horseshoes. I could hear them yelling and laughing and having fun as I pulled weeds. Oh, to be a little kid again, I thought, too little to know the difference between a weed and a vegetable.

Howard Kay and Jimmie Peterson came into the back yard as I stood up to relieve my aching back. Howard had a disappointed look on his pumpkin face. Jimmie hitched up his pants, which were too big for him. He didn't have any younger brothers to wear his hand-me-downs, so his mother

always bought him clothing that was one size too big.

"You told us to come over and play basketball this morning," Jimmie said.

For Christmas I'd been given the first basketball and backboard anybody in Adenville had ever seen. Papa had nailed the backboard to our coal and wood shed on the alley side.

"I forgot I had to weed the garden," I said.

"Shucks," Howard said.

Then I got a brilliant idea. "Help me weed the garden," I said, "and then we'll play."

Jimmie hitched up his pants again. "If we help you weed your garden will you help us weed our gardens?" he asked.

It wasn't such a brilliant idea after all. Jimmie's mother ran a boardinghouse and had a vegetable garden three times as big as ours.

"Forget it," I said. "The basketball is in the coal and wood shed."

By this time more kids were coming down the alley. In a few minutes I could hear the happy shouts of kids playing basketball and of Frankie and Eddie playing horseshoes. But there were no happy shouts for me. I was just a slave doomed to pull weeds while other kids had fun. And that afternoon while other kids were swimming in the nice cool river, I was still pulling weeds in the hot sun, my shirt wringing wet with sweat. Instead of happy shouts there were only groans coming from my lips because of my aching back.

The next day was Sunday. Bishop Aden announced during church services that there would be a town meeting in the Town Hall on Monday evening at eight o'clock. Reverend Holcomb made the same announcement at the Community Church. That afternoon Papa and Sweyn went to the *Advocate* office and printed handbills urging all adult citizens to attend the meeting. Monday morning Tom and I tacked the handbills to trees and light posts and put them in store windows on the east and west sides of town. For my money if anyone didn't know about the town meeting he had to be deaf, dumb, and blind.

Only adults were admitted to the meeting, but Papa told us about it during breakfast on Tuesday morning. The parents of thirty-three boys and girls had promised to enroll them at the Academy and pay a tuition fee of from thirty to forty dollars.

Papa told the audience the tuition money was just to pay a teacher's salary, and he called for donations to build and furnish the Academy. He began the donations by pledging five hundred dollars. Then Bishop Aden pledged the Church of Jesus Christ of Latter-day Saints would donate the land upon which to build the Academy and also pledged one thousand dollars. Mayor Whitlock, who was also president of the Adenville Bank, pledged five hundred dollars. Mr. Monaire, a big sheep rancher, pledged five hundred. I guess Mr. Pearson, who was a big cattle rancher, didn't want a sheepman outdoing a cattleman and he pledged five hundred. Mr. Daniels, the owner of the Fairplay Saloon, and Mr. Harper of the Whitehorse Saloon each gave five hundred dollars. And there were quite a few people who pledged from ten to one hundred dollars, and just about every able-bodied man in town volunteered to work for nothing to help build the school. Mayor Whitlock then made a motion that one Mormon, one Catholic, and one Protestant be elected as a board of directors to run the Academy. Bishop Aden, Papa, and Mayor Whitlock were elected. Mayor Whitlock became the chairman of the board of directors, Bishop Aden the treasurer, and Papa the secretary. Papa said Bishop Aden was leaving for Salt Lake City the next day to order the furniture, books, and school supplies, and also to arrange to hire a teacher.

"And," Papa said as he finished, "Mr. Jamison is working on blueprints for the building, and construction will start tomorrow." Then he looked across the table at Tom. "So, T.D., you won't be going to the Catholic Academy in Salt Lake City after all."

Tom had a funny expression on his face. I couldn't tell if he was disappointed or happy about it.

"Can they have the Academy ready by the time school starts?" he asked.

"Definitely," Papa said. "School won't start this year until Monday, September the fifth."

Mamma was smiling. "It is going to be wonderful having Tom D. home," she said to Papa.

Papa nodded. "After all the trouble he got into at the Jesuit Academy in Salt Lake City last year," he said, "it is going to be a relief having him where we can keep an eye on him."

All I can say is that for my money Papa had better keep a sharp eye on The Great Brain.

I'd seen many bees, as they were called in those days. We had barn-raising bees and house-raising bees where neighbors and friends pitched in to help a newly married couple build a house or barn. And we had corn-husking bees where friends and neighbors helped harvest corn, and any fellow who found a red ear of corn got to kiss the girl of his choice. We had a church-raising bee when the Community Church was built. But I'd never seen one like the Academy-raising bee.

It began on Wednesday morning. All the kids in town were on hand to watch after doing their morning chores. Mr. Jamison, the town's best carpenter and contractor, was bossing the job. Men were digging the trench for the foundation when we arrived. Women were spreading two picnic tables with baked beans, baked ham, fried chicken, bread and butter sandwiches, pies, cakes, and other good things to eat. Some Mormon women arrived with lemonade, cider, and cold milk in crocks. Mr. Daniels, the proprietor of the Fairplay Saloon, delivered a keg of beer, and so did Mr. Harper of the Whitehorse Saloon.

By noon the trench for the foundation of the building had been dug and some of the wooden forms for the concrete completed. The men working stopped to eat and drink, but only their wives and children could remain and eat after the men did. We had to go home for lunch. Just before we left, wagonloads of gravel and cement began to arrive.

Papa told us during lunch that he would be working on the Academy during the afternoon. "Mr. Jamison has decided to use two crews," he said, "one in the morning and a different one in the afternoon because so many men volunteered to help."

The *Advocate* office wasn't the only place of business that had a sign reading, CLOSED AT NOON—WORKING ON THE ACADEMY, that afternoon. I saw the same sign on several places of business.

Mr. Jamison was ready to start pouring concrete for the

foundation when we arrived. Papa and Danny's father, Mr. Forester, were given long sticks that Mr. Jamison called puddlers.

Frankie pointed at Papa. "Why is Papa pushing the stick up and down in the concrete?" he asked.

"To get the air out of the concrete so there won't be any air bubbles," Tom said, "and to help settle the concrete."

There was food for the afternoon crew too, and two more kegs of beer arrived from the saloons. That was one afternoon when not one kid in town went swimming. We watched until the last wheelbarrow of concrete had been poured for the foundation.

Papa told us during supper that it would take all night and all the next day and night for the concrete to cure.

Frankie looked at him. "Is the concrete sick?" he asked.

"No," Papa said, laughing. "To cure concrete means to wait for it to dry and harden."

The next morning Mr. Jamison was using only men with saws. They cut two-by-fours into studs, joists, and rafters until noon. There was nothing more that could be done on the Academy until the next morning when the forms on the concrete foundation could be removed. We watched the men begin building the frame for the Academy the next morning but went swimming that afternoon.

Fellows like Parley, Sammy, and Seth were very happy for the opportunity to get a seventh and eighth grade education. But it sure as heck made a few kids unhappy. Take a fellow like Danny Forester.

"I'm going to be a barber like my father," he told us at the swimming hole that afternoon. "My folks think I ought to get an education now that there's an academy right here in Adenville. But who needs more than a sixth grade education to learn how to give shaves and haircuts?"

Even Tom with his great brain couldn't answer that one.

I know it sounds silly, but I felt both happy and sad about the Academy. I was sad knowing Tom would blackmail and swindle me every chance he got instead of being at the Academy in Salt Lake City. I was unhappy knowing he had not really reformed and that sooner or later he would be caught swindling somebody who would tell. That would not only break Papa's and Mamma's hearts but also revoke his suspended sentence, and none of the fellows would have anything to do with him. I was happy knowing fellows like Parley, Seth, and Sammy would have a chance to make something of themselves. And I guess I was happy knowing Tom would remain at home, because with all his faults I loved him.

I asked Tom how he felt about the Academy as we walked home from the swimming hole with Frankie.

"I'm going to miss the good friends I made at the Jesuit Academy," he said. "But when I think of how strict the Jesuit priests were, I thank my lucky stars I'm not going back."

"Well," I said, "you had better keep your nose clean around here or Papa will send you back."

Tom seemed unconcerned. "With my great brain," he said, "I'll always be one step ahead of Papa and everybody else around here."

CHAPTER TWO

Tom and the Wild Jackass

MONDAY MORNING just a week before school was due to begin I went to Smith's vacant lot with Tom and Frankie to play. We were surprised to see only one kid there. My friend Howard Kay came running to meet us with an excited look on his pumpkin face.

"I waited for you," he shouted.

"Where are all the fellows?" Tom asked.

"At Parley's place," Howard said. "His father brought home three wild mares and a wild jackass last night. Mr. Benson is going to break the mares this morning."

Parley's father was a wild animal bounty hunter. Whenever cattlemen and sheepmen began losing livestock to wild animals they sent for Mr. Benson. He hunted down wolves, coyotes, mountain lions, and other wild animals that killed livestock. The ranchers paid him a bounty for each one he killed.

He had never bothered to capture wild horses before the 1890s. Thousands of wild horses roamed throughout the west during the 1800s, but it cost more to capture and break them than they were worth. But with the beginning of the Boer War the British government sent agents to the western states looking for horses to ship to South Africa. A sound animal broken to the saddle brought as much as forty dollars. This caused a shortage of work horses, roping horses, cutting horses, riding horses, and brood mares among the ranchers. Mr. Benson sold the wild stallions and mares he caught to the ranchers after breaking them. Us kids always hoped Mr. Benson would bring back mustangs because they were the hardest of all wild horses to break. They lived up to their Spanish name, which means "running wild."

The Bensons lived just inside the town limits. They had a big barn and corral in back of their house with a pasture beyond. There were about twenty kids sitting on the log railing of the pasture fence when we arrived. The wild mares were running around in the pasture trying to find a way out. The wild jackass was standing in the middle of the pasture. He sure didn't look wild to me. He looked as if he were asleep. He was a male which made him a jackass. The female burro is called a jennet or a jenny. Mr. Benson's big roan gelding, two pack mules, team of horses, and milk cow were grazing in the pasture not paying any attention to the wild mares or the jackass.

We climbed up on the fence and sat by Parley. He was wearing his coonskin cap that he would never take off outside unless he was about to go in swimming.

Tom stared at the burro. "Why did your father capture a wild jackass?" he asked.

"He didn't capture him," Parley said. "After Pa got the lead ropes on the three wild mares and started for home that jackass followed him. Pa reckons as how one of the mares could be his mate. The only way you get a mule is to breed a jackass to a horse mare."

"I know that," Tom said as if his great brain had been insulted. "How old is the jackass?"

"Pa figures about four years old," Parley answered.

"What is your father going to do with him?" Tom asked.

"He said I could have the jackass if I gentled him," Parley said.

"I know how you break a horse," Tom said. "But how do you gentle a jackass?"

"Same as a horse," Parley said. "Pa says all I've got to do is ride him and break his spirit and prove I'm the boss. Then it will be easy to break him to pack saddle and harness."

"You've got one of the best saddle ponies in town," Tom said. "You sure aren't going to be seen riding around on a dumb old jackass."

"Shucks, no," Parley said as he pushed his coonskin cap to the back of his head. "I'll sell him to a prospector or a trapper after I gentle him."

"When are you going to gentle him?" Tom asked.

"This afternoon," Parley answered.

Mr. Benson came to the pasture. He was a clean-shaven man with skin as tanned as the leather chaps he was wearing. He was wearing California spurs with two-inch rowels, which he used when breaking horses. We watched him lasso one of the wild mares with a leather lariat. He led the mare to the corral with all us kids following him. Parley helped his father get a bridle and saddle on the mare. He ran for the fence as Mr. Benson mounted the mare. She stood still, trembling, for a few seconds and then began to buck. But no wild mare can buck like a wild stallion. She only bucked for about two or three minutes and then gave up. Mr. Benson rode the mare around the corral a few times and then rode her back to the pasture. The other two mares were just as easy to gentle, so easy that Mr. Benson apologized to us.

"Sorry, boys," he said. "It wasn't much of a show. But maybe next time I'll get some wild stallions instead of mares."

Parley told us his father was leaving right after lunch to take the three mares to Pete Gunderson's ranch to sell and would stay at the ranch to do some bounty hunting.

"Don't try to gentle that wild jackass until we get here," Tom told Parley.

None of the kids went swimming that afternoon. We all went to watch Parley gentle the wild jackass. He had a halter on the burro in the corral when Tom, Frankie, and I arrived.

"Help me get a bridle on Chalky," Parley said to Tom.

"Chalky?" Tom asked.

"I named him Chalky because he is the color of chalk cliffs," Parley said.

They tried to get a bridle on the jackass, but Chalky refused to open his mouth and take the bit. Then they tried Parley's Morgan saddle on Chalky, but it was too big.

"I'll ride him bareback with just the halter," Parley said.

Tom shook his head. "At least put a girth around him to hold on to," he said.

They joined the girth from Parley's saddle to an extra strong girth Mr. Benson used for breaking horses. Tom held Chalky by the halter and one ear while Parley put the girth around the burro and tightened it. Then Tom handed Parley the rein rope of the braided rope halter and ran to climb on the top railing of the corral fence.

Parley jumped on Chalky's back holding the rein rope in his left hand and grabbing hold of the girth with his right hand. That wild jackass began to buck as if he were a wild mustang. He pitched Parley off his back in about ten seconds. He continued to buck for a couple of minutes. Then he stopped and looked at Parley who had run for the protection of the fence. And I'll be a six-legged jackass myself if Chalky didn't let go with a loud, "Hee haw," as if he were giving Parley the raspberry.

Danny Forester cupped his hands to his mouth. "Some broncobuster," he shouted. "Can't even ride a little burro!"

Parley went back inside the corral. He picked up his coonskin cap that he'd lost when he was bucked off. He walked up to Chalky with a determined look on his face, took the rein rope in his left hand, and grabbing the girth with his right hand, jumped on the jackass's back.

"Ride 'em, cowboy!" all of us kids watching began to yell.

We only got to yell, "Ride 'em, cowboy!" for about fifteen seconds before that wild jackass pitched Parley off his back. Parley got up limping. Some of the kids began giving him the raspberry as he walked to the fence. Then all the kids began laughing as Chalky let go with another loud,

"Hee haw." Parley's face turned red with embarrassment and anger.

"If you fellows think it's so funny," he said, "let me see you ride Chalky."

There were no volunteers.

"Are you all scared of a little burro?" Parley asked.

That was enough to make Tom, Basil Kokovinis, Danny Forester, and Seth Smith try to ride the wild jackass. He bucked them all off his back quicker than he had Parley. And he gave each one of them a loud, "Hee haw," after doing it, as if to let them know a dumb old jackass was smarter than a bunch of kids. We all sat on the corral fence staring at Chalky, who looked as if he were going to sleep. Finally Parley spoke.

"Pa says you have to ride them to break their spirit before you can break them to pack saddle and harness," he said. "Nobody can gentle that wild jackass. When Pa gets back I'm going to tell him to take Chalky back to Wild Horse Canyon and turn him loose."

"Don't give up so easy," Tom said.

"Who wouldn't give up?" Parley answered.

"I wouldn't," Tom said.

"Is that so?" Parley said. "Tell you what I'll do. I'll give that jackass to anybody who can ride him before Pa gets back."

Tom stared at Parley. "Do you really mean that?" he asked.

"Pa sure as heck ain't going to let me keep a jackass that I can't gentle and sell," Parley answered. "And I know if I can't ride him no kid in this town can ride him."

Parley wasn't boasting. Maybe he wasn't a broncobuster, but he could ride a horse better than any of the fellows. And with his pony, Blaze, he had won the trick-riding contest for kids his age at the county fair three years in a row.

That evening after supper as the family sat in the parlor Tom was quiet. Finally he spoke.

"Papa," he said, "how much is a male burro worth?"

"Not much," I said before Papa could answer. "Who would want a dumb old jackass?"

Papa dropped the magazine he was reading. "The question was addressed to me," he reprimanded me. "However, for your information, J.D., a burro is a lot smarter than a horse, as any prospector or trapper will tell you. If his load is too heavy, a burro will refuse to move until you lighten it. But a pack horse or mule will carry a load that he knows is too heavy for him. When a burro feels he has put in a day's work he will stop working and there isn't anything you can do to make him continue. But a horse will go on working until he drops from exhaustion if you make him. When the weather is hot a burro will slow down his pace and nothing can make him move any faster. But a horse will keep going at any pace you want him to go regardless of how hot it is."

Papa then looked at Tom. "To get back to your question," he said, "years ago during the gold and silver mining boom a burro was worth more than a horse because so many prospectors used them. But prospectors are few and far between today. I have noticed, however, that some trappers at the campgrounds prefer a burro to a pack mule or pack horse. But I doubt if you could get more than five dollars for one. Why do you ask?"

"Parley Benson has a wild jackass his father brought home," Tom said. "Parley said he would give the jackass to anybody who can ride him."

"I'm sure," Papa said, "that if Parley Benson can't ride that jackass you can't."

"Maybe my great brain can figure out a way to gentle that wild jackass," Tom said.

"Well just make certain you do it honestly," Papa said. "I don't want any backsliding out of you."

The next morning after chores Tom said he was going to talk to Mr. Blake who worked in Jerry Stout's saddle and harness shop. Mr. Blake had been a wild horse wrangler until a horse he was breaking fell on him leaving him too crippled to ride horses again. Mamma wanted me to run an errand to the store so I didn't go with Tom.

I was sitting on the back porch steps watching Frankie and Eddie Huddle play marbles when Tom returned.

"Why did you want to see Mr. Blake?" I asked as Tom sat down beside me.

"To find out if there was any other way to gentle a wild horse than trying to ride him," Tom answered. "Mr. Blake said the quickest and easiest way was to ride the horse and let him know you were his master by breaking his spirit. But there are two other ways. He said there are some wild mustangs and stallions who are such good bucking broncos that nobody can ride them. The only way to break their spirit is to put the horse in a stall and tie him so he can't buck. Then put heavy bags of dirt on the horse's back and beat him until you break his spirit."

"Boy, oh, boy," I said, "you wouldn't do that to a poor old jackass would you?"

"Of course not," Tom said as if I'd insulted him. "I'll use the third way and that is to make friends with the horse. Mr. Blake said if you let a wild horse know you are his friend and get him to like you, he will let you ride him without bucking."

"For my money," I said, "that wild jackass is too dumb to know he has any spirit to be broken and too stupid to know what a friend is."

"If my great brain can't figure out a way to make Chalky like me," Tom said, "I'll trade places with that jackass."

"Mamma and Papa wouldn't like it," I said.

"Like what?" Tom asked.

"Having Chalky living in our house," I said, "and you living in the Benson pasture." I thought that was very funny but Tom didn't even smile.

"I'm going up to my loft in the barn," he said, "and put my great brain to work on how to gentle Chalky."

Tom's great brain must have been working like sixty. He told me when he came down from the loft for lunch that he had a plan to gentle Chalky. He wouldn't tell me what the plan was until after lunch. Then he got some cubes of sugar from the kitchen and put them in his pocket. Frankie and I followed him into the backyard. He pulled up a bunch of carrots from the vegetable garden and washed them off under the hydrant. He laid them on the back porch to dry. Then he went into the house and got a brown paper bag.

"What's the idea?" I asked when he came to the porch.

"I want you and Frankie to go to Smith's vacant lot and go swimming with the fellows as usual," Tom said. "If they ask you where I am, tell them I'll be a little late getting to the swimming hole this week. Tell them Sweyn is leaving tomorrow to go back east to school and I have to start helping Papa at the *Advocate*."

"But Papa said he would only need you when he has a big printing job," I said. "He doesn't want anything to interfere with your school work when school starts Monday."

"So what?" Tom asked as if I was dumber than Chalky. "You won't be telling a lie if you tell them I have to start helping Papa at the *Advocate*."

"I'll tell the fellows," I said. "But I am also going to tell them that Frankie and I are going to wait for you. I want to be with you when you try to gentle Chalky."

"All right," Tom said, "but mum's the word for anything you see me do, and that goes for you too Frankie."

Frankie shook his head. "Nope," he said. "Eddie is coming over and I want to go swimming."

"We'll take you and Eddie swimming as soon as we get back," Tom said. "Now, J.D., go to Smith's vacant lot and tell the fellows. And make sure you wait until Parley is there."

I rode my bike toward Smith's vacant lot. I couldn't see anything wrong in helping Tom try to gentle the wild jackass. Parley had said he was going to have his father take Chalky back to Wild Horse Canyon and turn the jackass loose. And Parley had said anybody who could ride the jackass before his father returned could have Chalky. Either way Parley would have to give up the jackass. What difference did it make if Chalky was turned loose or Tom won him? There sure as heck wasn't anything dishonest in Tom's trying to gentle Chalky.

Parley and about fifteen other kids were at Smith's vacant lot when I arrived. I told them that Tom, Frankie, and I would be a little late and the reason why. But riding my bike back home my conscience bothered me a little. I'd told Parley and the other fellows a lie. Tom was waiting with the carrots in a paper bag when I returned.

"We'll walk," he said to me after telling Frankie and Eddie to wait for us.

We took a roundabout way to get to the Benson pasture so the kids at Smith's vacant lot couldn't see us. We didn't have to worry about Mrs. Benson seeing us because their big barn hid us from her backyard and home.

"You hide over there behind that tree," Tom said, "so Chalky won't notice you."

I did as he told me and then peeked around the trunk of the tree. Tom walked to the north end of the pasture. He climbed through the log rail fence and walked to the center of the pasture where Chalky was standing. I saw him reach into his pocket with his right hand while he held the bunch of carrots in his left hand. Then he held a cube of sugar under the jackass's mouth. Chalky's ears stood straight up as he nibbled the sugar cube from the palm of Tom's hand. I watched my brother feed Chalky three more cubes of sugar. Then Tom took half of the bunch of carrots and fed them to the jackass. When Chalky finished eating the carrots Tom held the other half in front of him and began walking toward the north side of the pasture fence. Again Chalky's ears stood up straight and he began following my brother. When Tom reached the fence he put the carrots on the ground for Chalky to eat. He patted the wild jackass on the neck and Chalky didn't seem to mind.

The next morning the whole family went down to the depot to see Sweyn off for Boylestown, Pennsylvania. Mamma didn't start to cry until the train was pulling out.

"It is so far away," she cried.

Papa put his arm around her shoulders. "Take comfort in knowing, dear," he said, "that because of the Adenville Academy we will have two of our sons and our adopted son home."

"But next year we will only have John D. and Frankie," Mamma said.

That afternoon I again went with Tom to the Benson pasture to watch from behind the tree. This time Tom left half the carrots by the north pasture fence. He fed Chalky lumps of sugar and then half the carrots. Then he took hold of the jackass's short mane. At first Chalky wouldn't move. Tom kept talking to the burro and finally Chalky let my brother lead him to the pasture fence where the other half of the carrots were.

Thursday afternoon we went back to the Benson pasture. Again Tom left half the carrots by the fence. Then he walked to the center of the pasture. He fed Chalky some cubes of sugar. Then, while Chalky was eating the carrots, Tom climbed on the burro's back. I watched Chalky's ears go flat back and thought for sure he would start to buck. But he didn't. He turned and looked at Tom and then continued eating. When he'd finished the carrots Chalky turned his head again to look at Tom, who was patting him on the neck and talking to him. I know Chalky couldn't understand what Tom was saying, but he must have remembered there were more carrots by the fence. He began to walk toward the north side of the pasture with Tom on his back. He found the carrots by the fence. While he was eating them Tom got off Chalky and after patting the burro on the neck and talking to him climbed through the fence and joined me.

"Your great brain did it," I said when we met.

"Chalky knows I'm his friend now and likes me," Tom said, "and tomorrow morning he will be all mine."

Later that afternoon we were sitting on the river bank at the swimming hole resting between swimming and diving when Danny and Parley sat down beside us.

"How is that wild jackass of yours?" Tom asked.

"As wild as ever," Parley said. "I tried riding him again Tuesday morning but he bucked me off twice."

"I'd like to take another crack at riding Chalky before your father gets back," Tom said. "How about tomorrow morning?"

Parley jumped to his feet and cupped his hands to his mouth. "Hey, all you kids!" he shouted. "Come over here!"

He waited until the fellows on the river bank and those who had been swimming were crowded around him.

"You are all invited to see The Great Brain dumped on his behind tomorrow morning," Parley said grinning. "He wants to try and ride Chalky again."

"I'll ride him," Tom said. "And when I do Chalky belongs to me. That was the deal you made."

Danny had something the matter with his left eyelid which was always half closed unless he was angry or excited. It flipped wide open as he stared at Tom.

"I'll bet you can't ride that wild jackass," he said.

Right away several other kids, including Parley, wanted to bet.

Tom shook his head. "You fellows know I can't bet any more now that I'm reformed," he said.

"But the other bets you made were all swindles," Parley said. "This can't be a swindle because there is no way your great brain could talk a wild jackass into letting you ride him. And if I can't ride Chalky I know darn well that you can't."

"I don't want to bet," Tom said.

Danny rammed a finger into Tom's chest. "You are afraid to bet because you know you will lose," he said.

"Wrong," Tom said. "I don't want to bet because I

know I'll win. You see, Danny, I know I can ride Chalky."

Parley spat. "What a sneaky way to get out of betting," he said.

"But I know I can ride Chalky," Tom said.

"And we are betting you can't," Parley said.

I figured it was up to me to stop Tom from swindling the fellows and backsliding. He would probably be very angry about it, but it was something I had to do.

"Don't bet, fellows," I said. "Tom can ride Chalky and when he does you'll lose your money and say you were swindled."

Danny pointed at me. "Now he has even got John trying to help him weasel out of betting," he said.

"Yeah," Parley said. "John knows Tom can't ride Chalky and is trying to save him."

"But I tell you he can," I protested.

"And we all say he can't," Parley said.

"Leave my brother out of this," Tom said. "If you fellows still want to bet tomorrow morning bring your money with you. I'll cover all bets."

Later as I walked toward home from the swimming hole I expected Tom to really be angry, but he didn't say anything.

"I was only trying to stop you from backsliding," I finally said. "You know you can ride Chalky. And when you do the fellows will claim it was a swindle and not have anything to do with you."

"I'm glad you said what you did," Tom said to my surprise. "It will make it even easier to prove it wasn't a swindle."

"For my money," I said, "it is an out and out swindle."

"Then your money must be counterfeit," Tom said.

We stopped at the Academy on our way home. The building was finished. Desks for the students and for the teacher were being carried into the building. We walked over and looked inside. Men were fastening the students' desks to the floor in the big classroom with screws. Papa was right. The Academy would be all finished before it was time for school to start.

The next morning after chores Tom dug up a bunch of carrots from our garden. He washed them off under the hydrant and swung them around to dry before putting them into a paper bag.

"Now, J.D.," he said, "I want you to help me teach those smarty pants a lesson. I'll go to the Benson corral and tell the fellows you had to run an errand. You sneak down to the north side of the pasture and put these carrots in the same spot by the fence where I put the others."

"No," I said. "Maybe I can't stop you from backsliding, but I'm not going to help you swindle the fellows."

"Not even for a quarter?" Tom asked.

"Not even for a dollar," I said.

"Suit yourself," Tom said. "I've plenty of time to do it myself."

I watched Tom leave knowing he was smart enough to plant the carrots without being seen by anybody. After what happened at the swimming hole the day before I knew it wouldn't do any good to tell the fellows not to bet. I went to the Benson corral with Frankie. There were about twenty kids there when we arrived.

Parley pushed his coonskin cap to the back of his head. "Where's Tom?" he asked. "Did he back out?"

"He'll be along," I said.

Tom arrived a few minutes later. He had a notebook, a pencil, and a paper bag. He told all the kids who wanted to make bets to line up. He wrote down the name of each fellow and the amount of his bet in the notebook. Then he made everyone put the money they had bet in the paper bag, which he covered with cash from his own pocket. He looked happier than I'd ever seen him since he'd reformed. I guess just getting back into action swindling kids was making his money-loving heart beat with joy. After all bets were made Tom handed me the notebook, pencil, and paper bag containing the money.

"You hold the stakes, J.D.," he said. "The bet is that I can't ride Chalky. And just to make it more interesting, I'm going to ride him in the pasture where he has more room to buck if he wants. And I'll ride him without the girth to hold on to." He turned to Parley. "Lend me your halter."

"Boy!" Parley exclaimed. "If I'd known you were going to try and ride Chalky without a girth I'd have bet fifty cents instead of just a quarter."

"It isn't too late to change your bet," Tom said.

"I ain't got any more spending money," Parley said.

Tom looked at the other kids. "Anybody want to raise their bet?" he asked. "I'm riding Chalky without the girth."

Four kids decided to raise their bets. After changing the bets in the notebook and putting the cash in the paper bag, we waited for Parley to get the halter from the barn. Then we all walked down to the pasture. Everybody except Tom climbed up on the top log railing of the fence. Tom opened the gate and stepped inside the pasture.

I watched Tom walk to where Chalky was standing in the center of the pasture. I knew that as he shielded the burro's head from our view with his back he was feeding

Chalky cubes of sugar. Then he put the halter on the jackass and climbed on Chalky's back.

Parley was staring bug-eyed. "Why don't he buck?" he said.

Chalky turned his head and looked at Tom. I guess he was wondering why he hadn't been given any carrots. Then he must have remembered that every time he'd been fed sugar there were carrots by the north side pasture fence. He started to walk and then broke into a trot until he reached the spot where Tom had placed the carrots. Tom jumped off Chalky's back. He patted the jackass on the neck. From where we were sitting it looked as if Chalky were just eating some of the pasture grass. Tom walked back across the pasture toward us. I knew he was just giving Chalky time to eat all the carrots.

All the kids except me and Frankie were staring at Tom with bulging eyeballs and open mouths. They couldn't have looked more surprised if The Great Brain had suddenly turned into a jackass himself.

Parley pointed at Tom. "You . . . you . . . you rode him and he didn't even buck," he stammered.

"We didn't bet on whether or not Chalky would buck," Tom said. "I bet I could ride him and I did, so I win all the bets made. And you said anybody who could ride the jackass could have him. And that means I now own Chalky."

"But why didn't he buck?" Parley asked as he and the rest of us kids jumped down from the fence.

"There is more than one way to gentle a jackass," Tom said, "when you have a great brain. I'll borrow your halter to take Chalky home with me and return it later."

Danny jumped in front of Tom. "No you won't," he said, "not until you give us our money back. You swindled us. You've been sneaking over here doing something to Chalky so he would let you ride him. You knew you could ride him when you bet."

"I told you all that I knew I could ride Chalky," Tom said.

"Yeah," Danny said, "but you've lied to us so many times to swindle us that you knew darn well we wouldn't believe you and that makes it a swindle." He turned and looked around at the other fellows. "I say Tom swindled us and if he doesn't give us our money back we won't have anything to do with him. All those in favor hold up their right hands."

Every kid who had made a bet held up his right hand. Somehow I knew this was going to happen. I felt sorry for Tom because he was my brother, but he knew what the penalty would be if he was caught backsliding. I knew it would break his money-loving heart to give back the two dollars and eighty cents he had won. But that was better than not having any of the fellows speak to him or play with him.

Danny turned to face Tom. "What's it going to be?" he asked. "Do you give us back our money or do we unsuspend your sentence or whatever they call it?"

Tom didn't even look worried. "The only person who can revoke my suspended sentence is the judge who sentenced me," he said. "You fellows say I swindled you. I say I didn't. We'll leave it up to Harold Vickers to decide who is right and who is wrong."

We all went to the Vickers home. Harold was the son of the district attorney and going to become a lawyer. That was why I'd asked him to be the judge at Tom's trial. His mother looked surprised when she saw about twenty kids on her big front porch when she opened the door after Tom had knocked. She said Harold was in his room and busy.

"It is very important, Mrs. Vickers," Tom said. "Please call him."

Harold looked annoyed when he came to the front porch wearing his glasses with the thick lenses. "What do you kids want?" he asked. "I'm busy packing and getting ready to leave on the morning train to go back to high school in Salt Lake City."

Tom explained about Parley's offering Chalky to anybody who could ride him and about betting the fellows that he could ride the jackass.

"I rode the jackass," Tom continued, "and won two dollars and eighty cents from the fellows who bet. Now they say I swindled them and want you to revoke my suspended sentence."

Harold looked around at the fellows. "I haven't time to hear each one of you give testimony," he said. "Choose one of you to act as spokesman for the group."

Danny stepped forward. "I'll do it," he said. "Tom knew he could ride the jackass when he made the bets and that makes it a swindle."

Harold looked at Tom. "That sounds as if you did swindle them," he said.

"Your honor," Tom said, "according to the dictionary and the law a swindle is getting money or property from somebody by fraud or deceit. Am I right?"

"That is true," Harold said.

"And according to the dictionary and the law a fraud is tricking somebody into giving you something by lying to them," Tom said. "Am I right?"

"You are," Harold said.

"Well, your honor," Tom said, "I didn't deceive or lie to anybody. I told the fellows that I knew I could ride the jackass before we made any bets."

Harold turned to Danny. "Is that true?" he asked.

"Well, yes," Danny admitted. "But we thought he was lying."

"Your honor," Tom said, "it is not my fault they didn't believe me when I told them I knew I could ride the jackass. And Parley offered to give the jackass to anybody who could ride him. He didn't say I couldn't gentle the jackass by making friends with it. So how can anybody say I swindled them?"

Harold thought for a moment. "The court rules," he said, "the defendant did not use fraud or deceit and therefore is not guilty of swindling anybody. The sentence remains suspended. And if you kids were stupid enough to bet after he told you he knew he could ride the jackass, you were jackasses yourselves for betting. Court is adjourned."

The fellows were very quiet as we walked back to the Benson place. I didn't know if it was because The Great Brain had made fools out of them or because they had lost their money betting. Tom borrowed a halter and rode Chalky to our corral with me and Frankie following on foot. He didn't have any trouble when he put our packsaddle on the jackass. It was too big, but the burro let Tom lead him around the corral a few times carrying the packsaddle. Then Tom removed it and motioned to me.

"Now J.D.," he said, "I want to make sure Chalky knows human beings are his friends before I sell him. Get on him and ride him around the corral a few times."

I figured that wild jackass might be Tom's friend but

that didn't mean he was mine. "I don't feel like getting pitched off on my behind," I said.

"I tell you he won't buck," Tom said. "He's plumb gentled."

"I would rather Chalky told me," I said.

"If you are afraid," Tom said, "I'll let Frankie ride him."

That was enough to force me to ride the jackass. I sure as heck didn't want to be known as a fellow who was afraid to do something his six-year-old brother wasn't afraid to do. I got on Chalky. He didn't buck. I rode him around the corral a few times. Then Frankie wanted to ride the burro. Tom let him until Mamma called us for lunch.

After eating I went to the campgrounds with Tom to sell Chalky. The streams in the mountains around Adenville had a lot of beaver dams in them. Trappers who caught beaver and other wild animals for their furs always came to Adenville for provisions. It was closer to the beaver dams than any other town. There were usually three or four trappers at the campgrounds. But when we arrived there was just one, a man named Brussard. He said he didn't need a burro but knew another trapper who did. After some haggling Tom sold Chalky for six dollars.

"I'll bet," I said as we left the campgrounds, "that he sells Chalky for more than six dollars."

"I don't believe he would cheat a friend," Tom said.

"Speaking of cheating," I said, "boy, oh, boy, are you backsliding."

Tom grabbed my arm and spun me around. "And just what do you mean by that?" he asked.

"For my money," I said, "you were betting on a sure

thing when you bet you could ride Chalky, which makes it a swindle even if you did pull the wool over Harold's eyes."

"I proved it wasn't a swindle," Tom said, "and Harold as the judge agreed. Now along comes my own flesh and blood and accuses me of being a swindler and backslider. I think we will just let Mamma and Papa settle this. I'll tell my side of the story and you tell yours. I'm sure they will decide in my favor and punish you for calling your own brother a swindler and backslider."

Boy, oh, boy, my little brain and big mouth had done it again. I knew with that dictionary business and with Harold agreeing it wasn't a swindle, that Tom could easily convince our parents he hadn't swindled anybody. And I knew my punishment would be the loss of my allowance for at least a month and the silent treatment. Other kids in town just got a whipping when being punished. Our parents punished us by taking away our allowance and giving us the silent treatment which was ten times worse than a whipping. It meant that Papa and Mamma wouldn't speak to us and would practically pretend we didn't exist for a day, a week, or even longer, depending upon what we had done.

"I'm sorry I called you a backslider and swindler," I said.

"I'm not going to let you off with just an apology," Tom said as he took a penny from his pocket and handed it to me.

"What's that for?" I asked staring at the penny.

"Mamma wants the vegetable garden weeded again tomorrow," Tom said. "I'm paying you one cent to weed my share."

"Oh, no, you don't," I said. "I'm not weeding your half for just a penny."

"Would you rather I tell Papa and Mamma that you

called me a backslider and swindler?" Tom asked.

"I'll weed the garden," I said, knowing he had me over a barrel. "But why the penny?"

"So Mamma and Papa won't be suspicious when you tell them you are going to weed the garden by yourself," Tom said. "All you've got to do is to tell them I paid you to weed my share of the garden and you won't be telling a lie. You don't have to tell them how much I paid you."

"Thanks," I said, but I sure as heck didn't feel grateful.

I knew The Great Brain had swindled the fellows out of two dollars and eighty cents. I knew he had blackmailed me into weeding the garden again. He was still the same old swindler, crook, confidence man, and blackmailer he had always been. His great brain and money-loving heart would never let him reform. And tomorrow, the last Saturday before school started, other kids would be playing and going swimming and having fun while I pulled weeds all day. I felt so down in the dumps that I wished I had three legs. Then I could run around the block on two legs and use the other one to kick myself all the way for not having sense enough to keep my big mouth shut.

CHAPTER THREE

The Train Robbery

SCHOOL STARTED ON MONDAY morning. Kids who had gone barefooted most of the summer now had to wear shoes. Faces had to be scrubbed shiny. Uncomfortable clothing had to be worn. Mr. Standish was still the master of the first through the sixth grades in the common school. Mr. Harvey Monroe became the master of the seventh and eighth grades at the Academy. Lessons had to be learned. Books had to be studied. Homework had to be done. It was like going to prison after the carefree summer vacation, and enough to make a fellow sit right down and bawl.

Papa asked Tom what he thought of Mr. Monroe during supper after our first day of school.

"I guess he will be all right," Tom said after swallowing a mouthful of pot roast. "But he is very young to be a teacher."

"He graduated from the University of Utah last June," Papa said. "This is his first teaching contract."

"That explains it," Tom said. "He sure was nervous his first day."

School always began at the same time the ranchers were rounding up cattle for market. Papa received an advertisement every fall from the Bruford Brothers Meat-Packing Company in Kansas City. He ran the advertisement just about when school started. This year he published it in the September 6 edition of the *Advocate,* the day after school began. The advertisement notified all cattlemen that Mr. Paul Simpson would be in Adenville during the week beginning September 11 to buy cattle for the company.

When the advertisement appeared the cattle ranchers started rounding up beef animals for market—mostly four- and five-year-old steers and older dry cows. The ranchers brought the cattle to Adenville a day or two before Mr. Simpson was due to arrive. They put them in the livestock loading pens by the railroad spur track. From there the cattle would be shipped by rail to Kansas City.

All the ranchers liked dealing with Mr. Simpson because he always offered a fair price for cattle. He treated the small ranchers with just a few head to sell the same as the big ranchers with a hundred or more head to sell. I guess that was why cattle buyers from other meat-packing companies very seldom came to Adenville.

The Saturday after our first week of school every kid in town was down at the loading pens. We watched drovers for big ranches like the Flying W put their cattle in large separate pens. The smaller ranchers with just a few head of cattle to sell put their cattle all together in a big pen. When the sale of the cattle belonging to each small rancher began, cowboys on cutting horses would separate the cattle belonging to each rancher by the brands on them and run them through the chute to be tallied.

Monday morning it was back to school again. The Academy was just two blocks from the common school. Frankie, who was in the first grade, waited with me for Tom at noon and after school. When we arrived home for lunch that day Mamma told us Papa wouldn't be eating with us.

"Why not?" Tom asked.

"He hung up the telephone before I could ask him," Mamma said. "Then I remembered that Mr. Simpson is due to arrive on the eleven o'clock train this morning. Your father always has lunch with Mr. Simpson at the Sheepmen's Hotel while getting news about the cattle business."

When Tom, Frankie, and I got home from school that afternoon Mamma and Aunt Bertha were in the kitchen making Parker House rolls for supper. We always had a glass of milk and some cookies after school before changing into our play clothes. I could see Mamma was upset about something.

"All I can say, Bertha," she was saying as we entered the kitchen, "is that it is a fine how-do-you-do when the wife of the editor and publisher of the *Advocate* has to find out about a train robbery second hand."

"A train robbery!" Tom shouted. "Where? When?"

"The eleven o'clock train was held up twenty-five miles north of town," Mamma said, "and poor Mr. Simpson was killed by the robbers. But did I find out about it from your father? No. I learned about it from Mrs. Smith, who heard about it from Mrs. Olsen, who heard about it from Mrs. Larson. And when I finally reached your father at the *Advocate* office he said he would tell us all about it when he came home for supper."

"I'm not waiting," Tom said, with an excited look on his freckled face. "I'm going to the *Advocate* office."

"No, you aren't," Mamma said sharply. "Your father said he was very busy, and that means he doesn't want to be disturbed."

We were all waiting in the parlor when Papa arrived home for supper. I expected to hear Mamma really tell Papa off for not letting her know about the train robbery. But she didn't. She smiled and kissed him as she always did.

Tom looked as if he was going to explode with curiosity. "The train robbery!" he exclaimed. "What about the train robbery?"

Papa sat down in his rocking chair. "I had to tear down the front page of tomorrow's edition of the *Advocate*," he said, "and set type for the story of the train robbery and the murder of Mr. Simpson. The type is all set and ready for the Washington press. I'll have to work tonight."

Then Papa told us what had happened. Nels Larson, the stationmaster, had received the usual telegram from the stationmaster at Cedar City that the train had left there on time. This meant the train should arrive in Adenville at eleven o'clock. Mr. Larson waited until eleven thirty and then telephoned Uncle Mark. He told my uncle the train must have been in a wreck from a rock slide or something or it would have been on time. Uncle Mark got Dr. LeRoy, Papa, and some other men to organize a rescue party. By the time they had blankets, medicine, shovels, and everything needed for a train wreck loaded into a wagon, the train pulled into the station almost an hour and a half late. Uncle Mark quickly interviewed trainmen and passengers and then left with a posse. Papa interviewed trainmen and passengers and went to the *Advocate* to write the story and set type for it.

"The outlaws stopped the train by pulling logs across the tracks," Papa continued. "None of the trainmen were armed because we've never had a train robbery between here and Salt Lake City. One of the outlaws held a gun on the engineer and the fireman. The other three entered the passenger coach. The leader of the gang must have known Simpson on sight and that the cattle buyer was carrying a large amount of cash. Simpson was armed, like most cattle buyers. He tried to draw his gun and was killed. The outlaws took Simpson's money belt and made their escape. They took the engineer and fireman with them for about three miles and made the men walk back. That is why the train was so late getting here."

Papa stopped talking and began shaking his head. "I just can't believe it," he said.

"Believe what?" Mamma asked.

"I just can't believe it was Butch Cassidy and the Wild Bunch," Papa said. "Cassidy has never killed a man during a robbery and never operated around southwestern Utah."

No wonder Papa found it hard to believe. Butch Cassidy was known as the Robin Hood of the west because he robbed the rich and gave to the poor. His real name was George Leroy Parker. He was born in Circleville when Utah was still a territory. The Wild Bunch committed robberies from Canada to Mexico and from Nebraska to California. But they spent most of their time in Utah at a place known as Brown's Hole or another place called Robbers' Roost near Hanksville, Utah. The rugged terrain of both places made it

just about impossible to capture the gang—not that any posse tried very hard. Papa often said Cassidy had so many friends among legitimate people that a marshal or sheriff couldn't get enough volunteers to make up a posse. Butch Cassidy and his gang were often seen in Hanksville, but the marshal made no attempt to arrest them. Cassidy and his gang had helped so many people in the town and spent so much money there that the townspeople would have probably tarred and feathered anybody who tried to arrest them.

Cassidy had the distinction of being the only outlaw who attended his own funeral alive. An outlaw identified as Cassidy had been killed at San Rafael Swell south of Price, Utah. Cassidy, concealed in a covered wagon, rode down Main Street in Price and saw what was supposed to be his body lying in state. Later it was discovered that the dead man was really a minor outlaw named Jim Herron who looked like Cassidy.

Mamma was the first to recover from her surprise. "Then how can you say it was Butch Cassidy and the Wild Bunch?" she asked.

"Sam Ludell was on the train returning from a vacation in Salt Lake City," Papa said. "He identified the leader as Butch Cassidy."

"And just who is Sam Ludell?" Mamma asked.

"He is a blackjack dealer at the Fairplay Saloon," Papa answered. "Before coming here about a year ago, Ludell worked in a saloon at Castle Gate. He was there when Cassidy and the Wild Bunch stole the mine payroll. You remember me printing the story in the *Advocate* about how Cassidy, posing as a cowboy, hung around Castle Gate for a week getting the lay of the land before the robbery. He drank and played poker in the saloon where Ludell was working during that week. That is how Ludell knew him."

Tom shook his head. "Didn't the outlaws wear masks?" he asked.

"They all had red bandanna handkerchiefs tied over their noses," Papa said.

"Then how could Sam Ludell identify Butch Cassidy?" Tom asked.

"If you will just refrain from asking so many questions," Papa said, "I will tell you. Paul Simpson was sitting in a seat by himself. Ludell was sitting by himself in a seat across the aisle from Simpson. Ludell said the leader of the outlaws leaned over and ripped open Simpson's shirt with his left hand, while holding a gun on the cattle buyer in his right hand. He motioned for Simpson to remove the money belt and hand it over. Instead Simpson tried to draw his gun and the outlaw shot him. Then in a dying gesture Simpson reached up and pulled down the bandanna handkerchief. Ludell claims that during the couple of seconds it took the outlaw to pull the bandanna back up that he got a good enough look at the outlaw's face to identify him as Butch Cassidy."

Papa paused for a moment as he again shook his head. "Then there is Mrs. Parker's story that corroborates Ludell's story," he said. "She was returning from visiting her sister in Cedar City. She claims that just before Simpson was shot she heard him say, 'Butch.' Now it is entirely possible that Simpson had seen Cassidy in person at some time or seen wanted posters of the outlaw. And it is also possible that he recognized the outlaw even with the face partly covered by the bandanna handkerchief. And it is also possible that

Simpson, knowing Cassidy had never killed a man during a holdup, dared to go for his gun. All these things are possible. But I won't believe Butch Cassidy killed Simpson unless Mark and the posse bring him back."

Papa then looked at Mamma. "How about some supper now, Tena," he said. "I didn't have any lunch."

After supper Papa said he wanted Tom and me to go to the *Advocate* office and help him. Papa operated the Washington press while Tom fed newsprint into it. I folded the newspapers and put the yellow mailing stickers on the ones to be mailed. Papa told me to hand print a mailing sticker and send a copy of the paper to the editor of the *Hanksville Bugle*. It was almost ten before we went to bed. I was very sleepy but there was one question that suddenly began to bother me.

"Why do cattle buyers carry such large sums of cash?" I asked Tom as we started to get undressed.

"Because it has always been the custom for cattle buyers to pay in cash," Tom answered, "so the ranchers get their money right on the spot."

"How much do you figure Mr. Simpson had in his money belt?" I asked.

"There must be five hundred head of cattle in the loading pens," Tom said. "That is about the same as last year. At ten dollars a head that would be five thousand dollars. I would guess that Mr. Simpson, not knowing just how many head of cattle there would be, must have been carrying about six thousand dollars."

"Boy, oh, boy," I said. "That is a lot of money. Why don't you put your great brain to work on solving the train robbery and murder? I'll bet the Bruford Brothers would give you a big reward if you did."

"I might do just that," Tom said, "if Uncle Mark and the posse don't catch the outlaws."

Uncle Mark and the posse didn't catch the outlaws. They returned the same night because they didn't have a chance of tracking them. Papa told us about it during lunch the next day. Southwestern Utah has several large lava beds left by extinct volcanoes. Just a few miles from the train robbery the outlaws had crossed one of them, leaving no tracks. Uncle Mark and the posse circled the lava bed trying to find out where the outlaws left it. They failed because the lava bed was surrounded by desert and the wind was blowing. Early Mormon pioneers complained to their leader Brigham Young about the wind in Southwestern Utah. They said they had to plant a seed and stand on it until it rooted or the wind would blow it away. The wind had erased all tracks wherever the outlaws had left the lava bed.

After lunch Tom told Frankie and me he was going to the depot to talk to Mr. Larson the stationmaster about the train robbery. Frankie and I went on to the common school. We met Tom on the corner when school let out.

"I've decided to put my great brain to work on the train robbery and the murder of Mr. Simpson," he told us. "Tell Mamma I've gone to talk to Uncle Mark."

"Can I come?" I asked.

"All right," Tom said. "But Frankie, you tell Mamma that J.D. and I won't be home until it is time to do the chores."

Tom and I went to the marshal's office. It was called the marshal's office because Sheriff Baker was so seldom there. It was really a combination of the marshal's and sheriff's office and the jail. When the old marshal's office had burned down years before, Uncle Mark was made a deputy sheriff as well as marshal and had used the office ever since. He was sitting at his desk with his Stetson hat pushed to the back of his head and staring at the ceiling. There were no prisoners in any of the three cells.

"I was just thinking," he said, "it seems as if every time something serious happens around here Sheriff Baker is out of town."

"That is why they made you a deputy sheriff," Tom said.

"It's a big county," Uncle Mark said. "Sheriff Baker has a lot of territory to cover, but I do expect him back tomorrow."

One thing I always liked about Uncle Mark. He never talked down to Tom and me. He treated us as if we were grownups.

"I put my great brain to work on the train robbery," Tom said as we sat down. "I don't believe Butch Cassidy and the Wild Bunch did it."

Uncle Mark looked at Tom with interest. "Why?" he asked.

"Because Cassidy has never killed a man during a robbery," Tom said, "and because he and his gang have never operated around here."

"I doubt that it was Cassidy and his gang too," Uncle Mark said. "But I've got a little more to go on than you do."

"What?" Tom asked.

"You will both have to promise anything I say won't go any farther than the walls of this office," Uncle Mark said.

Tom and I both promised.

Uncle Mark leaned back in his chair. "This train robbery was planned by somebody who knows this part of the country well," he said. "Only somebody familiar with the area and knowing how strong the wind blows around here would have picked that particular place near the lava bed to hold up the train. And the leader of the gang was somebody who knew Simpson would be on the train and who also knew the cattle buyer on sight."

"I can't understand why Mr. Simpson was foolish enough to go for his gun," Tom said, "when the leader of the outlaws had a gun pointed straight at him."

"It doesn't make sense to me either," Uncle Mark said. "But that is what Sam Ludell said happened. No other passenger in the coach could have seen it."

"If Sam Ludell recognized Butch Cassidy why didn't the outlaw recognize him?" Tom asked.

"Ludell claims he saw Cassidy drinking and playing draw poker in the saloon in Castle Gate where he worked," Uncle Mark said. "Claims Cassidy never noticed him because he was the blackjack dealer and the outlaw never played blackjack."

"What do you think really happened?" Tom asked.

"I believe Simpson recognized the man who killed him," Uncle Mark said. "It might have been from the clothing the man was wearing—a ring on his finger or something like that. And I think Simpson was so surprised that he blurted out the man's name. The outlaw, knowing he'd been recognized, had to kill Simpson. And I believe Mrs. Parker heard the name Simpson spoke. But as soon as the outlaws left Ludell jumped up and began shouting it was Butch Cassidy. And poor frightened Mrs. Parker imagined the name she heard was Butch. It might have been a name that didn't even sound like Butch."

"Why do you think Mr. Ludell insists it was Butch Cassidy he saw?" Tom asked.

"He was working in Castle Gate when Cassidy and the Wild Bunch stole that mine payroll at the depot there," Uncle Mark said. "I think when the train was held up the first thing that popped into his mind was the mine payroll holdup. And it is possible the outlaw did look like Cassidy. Put them all together and Ludell is convinced it was Cassidy."

"Thanks, Uncle Mark," Tom said as we stood up. "See you later."

"Hold it," Uncle Mark said. "If you get any kind of a lead you must bring it to me. These men are wanted for murder and robbery. They have killed one man and wouldn't hesitate to kill again, even a boy, rather than get caught. Promise?"

"I promise," Tom said.

We left the marshal's office and started for home.

"You know, J.D.," Tom said, "I think Uncle Mark is right about everything except for one thing."

"What's that?" I asked.

"He said Mrs. Parker might have heard a name that didn't even sound like Butch," Tom said. "But no matter how frightened she was I don't think Mrs. Parker would have said it was Butch, even with Ludell yelling it was Butch Cassidy, unless the name she heard did sound like Butch."

"How do you figure that?" I asked.

"What if the name Mrs. Parker heard was a name like Bill or Harry or Steve?" Tom asked. "She would know darn well it wasn't Butch no matter how frightened she was. My great brain tells me that it has to be a name that sounds like Butch."

Uncle Mark received a telegram from the Bruford Brothers after we'd left him. He stopped and showed it to Papa who told us about it when he came home for supper.

"They asked Mark to arrange with the local undertaker to ship Mr. Simpson's body to Kansas City for burial," Papa said. "They also asked him to notify the ranchers who have cattle to sell that they are sending another cattle buyer named Harold Perkins to take Mr. Simpson's place. But Mr. Perkins won't be able to arrive in Adenville until Saturday. I don't believe the ranchers will complain though, because the Bruford Brothers have agreed to foot the bill for hay to feed the cattle until Mr. Perkins arrives. They also asked Mark to hold Mr. Simpson's personal possessions and give them to Perkins to take back to Kansas City with him."

After supper Tom, Frankie, and I did our homework. Then Frankie and I began playing checkers sitting on the floor in front of the parlor fireplace. Tom came into the room with a pencil and notebook. He sat in a chair, wrote down a word, and stared at it. Then he wrote some more words and stared at them. Even Papa became curious.

"What are you writing in that notebook that is so interesting?" he asked.

"I'm trying to find a name that sounds like Butch," Tom said. "I've found words like clutch, crutch, much, such, and touch. But the only name I can think of is Dutch. Do you know anybody called Dutch?"

"Yes," Papa said. "Dutch Wegland. He is an old-time prospector. Comes into town about twice a year looking for a grub stake. But Dutch is an old man now in his seventies and a loner and not the type of person who would rob a train."

Tom shook his head. "Mr. Simpson sure as heck wouldn't say a word like crutch before being shot," he said.

"I don't know about that," Papa said. "A man facing death is liable to say anything. I remember when Hank Davis was hung in Silverlode after being convicted of murder. The last thing he ever said was, 'trees.' No doubt about it. The marshal and hangman heard him say 'trees' just before the trap was sprung."

Tom shut the notebook. "I give up," he said.

Papa studied Tom for a moment. "I know there is something you aren't telling me," he said, "because you gave up too easily. I think I know what it is. Sheriff Baker will be back tomorrow or the next day. I suggest you leave the train robbery up to him and your Uncle Mark."

And that for my money was like telling a kid who has just bought an ice cream cone to throw it away.

CHAPTER FOUR

Tom and the Numbers Trick

TOM SURPRISED FRANKIE and me by going up to bed at the same time we did that night.

"How come you are going to bed an hour early?" I asked as we entered the bedroom.

"Yeah, how come?" Frankie said.

"My great brain has to figure out how it would be possible to recognize somebody who is masked," Tom said.

"Uncle Mark said it could be a ring on a finger or the clothing the outlaw was wearing," I said.

"I don't think so," Tom said. "Nobody would be dumb enough to wear a ring or clothing they knew would be recognized. I'm going to try an experiment."

The Great Brain got a bandanna handkerchief from his dresser drawer. He put it over his nose and tied it around in back of his head. Then he got a hat from the clothes closet and put it on.

"Now, you two take a good look at me," he said. "How do you know it is me?"

"Who else could it be?" I asked.

"Yeah, who else?" Frankie said.

"If you didn't know it was me," Tom said, "how would you guess it is me?"

"From the clothing you are wearing," I said, showing him I wasn't a dumbbell.

"Now imagine that I'm wearing clothing you've never seen," Tom said. "How would you know it was me?"

I stared at him for a couple of minutes. "The only way I could guess it might be you would be from the freckles on your high cheekbones and forehead. But lots of kids have freckles."

Tom removed the bandanna and hat. "This is a tough one," he said, "but there has to be an answer."

Frankie got between us. "I'd know it was you even if you covered up all your face."

Tom dropped to his knees and put his hands on Frankie's shoulders. "How would you know?"

"By the scar on your hand," Frankie said.

Tom removed his left hand from Frankie's shoulder and stared at it. He had given himself a nasty cut with a knife he was using to top beets from our garden before Frankie came to live with us. It had left a scar on the back of his hand about two inches long. He gave Frankie a little hug.

"Thanks, Frankie," he said. "Now we are getting somewhere."

The next day after school we went home and changed clothes. Eddie Huddle came over to play with Frankie. Tom and I sat on the back porch steps. I knew his great brain was working like sixty as he kept staring at the scar on his hand.

"Got it!" he said, jumping to his feet. "I'm going to the barber shop. Maybe Mr. Forester can give me a clue."

"Can I come?" I asked.

"If you keep your mouth shut no matter what I say," Tom answered.

Mr. Forester was alone in his barber shop when we got there. He was standing before the back mirror staring at his bald head. Papa sometimes joked about Mr. Forester because the barber bought every new hair tonic he saw advertised that was supposed to grow hair. But he still had just a fringe of hair around the edges and a big bald spot on top. For my money Papa had a lot of nerve, because our attic was filled with crazy inventions Papa had seen advertised and bought. And none of them worked.

Mr. Forester had never been friendly with Tom because The Great Brain had swindled his son Danny so many times. But he was very friendly now believing Tom had reformed.

"Hello, Tom and John," he said. "I know you aren't here for a haircut because I gave both of you a haircut just before school started. What can I do for you?"

"We came to ask you a question to settle a bet," Tom said.

Mr. Forester frowned. "I thought you gave up betting when you reformed," he said.

Tom showed him the scar on his hand. "We aren't betting money," he said. "J.D. and I got to talking about people who have scars on their hands and faces. I bet him that you could name ten men in town who had scars because you are a barber."

"I can name you several men who have scars on their faces," Mr. Forester said, "but not on their hands. I have to watch the scars on the faces of men I shave. Hal Benson has a scar on his right cheek, Fred Harvey on his chin, Matt Gillis just under his right eye, Jerry Stout on his cheek, Lem Carter a nasty scar on his throat, and Frank Collopy a scar on his nose. Reckon you lose the bet, Tom, because I can't think of any more offhand."

"How about people living on farms and ranches?" Tom asked.

"Let me see," Mr. Forester said. "Peter Gunderson and Charlie Smedly have cheek scars. And Dave Ecord's whole face is scarred. Got it from being kicked by a horse. Wonder it didn't kill him. Gave a shave and a haircut to two more just yesterday, Grant and Hutchinson from the Flying W ranch. Couple of wild ones those two buckeroos. Herb Grant has a scar from a knife fight that split his lips, and Hutch has a scar over his right eyebrow and just above it. Got hit with a broken bottle in a saloon fight one night."

"Thank you very much," Tom said.

We ran all the way to the marshal's office. Sheriff Baker had returned and was sitting at his desk. He was a very big man, taller and heavier and quite a bit older than Uncle Mark. He had the biggest gray walrus mustache of any man in town.

"Howdy, boys," he said. "If you are looking for your uncle he will be back in a few minutes."

"I guess Uncle Mark told you all about the train robbery and murder of Mr. Simpson," Tom said as we sat down.

"Yep," Sheriff Baker said. "Figure your uncle is right

about it not being Butch Cassidy and the Wild Bunch."

We talked about the train robbery until Uncle Mark arrived a few minutes later. He said hello to Tom and me and then spoke to the sheriff.

"Checked the livery stable," he said. "No horses were rented out the morning of the train robbery. Wouldn't have done us much good anyway. The outlaws hid the horses behind some trees and bushes."

"Didn't the engineer and fireman get a look at the brands on the horses when the outlaws took them along?" Sheriff Baker asked.

"Couldn't," Uncle Mark said. "The outlaws blindfolded them and told them not to look back when they let them go."

"Just another thing that indicates it must have been somebody around here who did the job," Sheriff Baker said. "They were afraid somebody on the train from Adenville might recognize one or more of the horses."

Tom stood up. "If I can help you find the outlaws will I get the reward?" he asked.

Sheriff Baker leaned forward in his chair. "Your uncle has told me some fantastic stories about that great brain of yours," he said. "You help us catch and convict these outlaws and you can have any reward money there might be."

"First," Tom said, "what can you tell me about a man named Hutchinson who works at the Flying W ranch?"

"He is the nephew of Fred Pearson who owns the ranch," Sheriff Baker said. "His mother died when the boy was just a youngster and his father was killed in an accident soon after. Pearson took the boy in to raise and spoiled him rotten. Your uncle can tell you more about that than I can."

Uncle Mark sat down at his desk. "Ever since he was old enough to enter a saloon," he said, "Hutch has been nothing but trouble. He started a saloon fight every time he came to town and he began gambling and running up debts. His uncle paid for the damages and the fines and settled the gambling debts for about three years. Then about a month ago I guess Pearson got fed up. He notified the saloon keepers he wouldn't be responsible for any more of his nephew's gambling debts. And he told Judge Potter and me he would let his nephew rot in jail before he would pay any more fines." Uncle Mark shook his head. "But I knew it wouldn't last."

"Why do you say that?" Tom asked.

"Because Hutch has been gambling and losing heavily at the Fairplay Saloon for the past two nights," Uncle Mark answered.

"Just one more question," Tom said, "and I think my great brain will have the train robbery solved. Mr. Simpson would know Hutchinson, wouldn't he?"

"Of course," Uncle Mark said. "Hutch has been coming into town with his uncle since he was about sixteen to tally cattle sold to Simpson." Then Uncle Mark came out of his chair as if he had been sitting on a tack. "I know what you are leading up to but go on."

"You called him Hutch," Tom said. "And Mr. Forester called him Hutch. And there is nobody around here with a name that sounds like Butch except him. And Mr. Forester said Hutch had a scar over his left eyebrow. A scar like that could be seen above a bandanna mask. I think Mr. Simpson recognized Hutch by the scar, and what Mrs. Parker heard him say before he was shot was Hutch and not Butch. And Hutch, knowing he'd been recognized, had to kill Mr. Simpson. And if Mr. Pearson isn't making his nephew's gambling debts good, that must mean that the money Hutch is losing playing poker was stolen from Mr. Simpson."

Uncle Mark turned to Sheriff Baker. "Tom could be right," he said.

"It is a damn good theory," Sheriff Baker said. "And while we are at it let's get Calvin Whitlock to keep a record of all Kansas City bank notes deposited in his bank. If local people pulled this train robbery the money will start burning a hole in their pockets, and they will start spending it. Simpson has always paid for cattle with Kansas City bank notes. About the only time they show up around here is when he is in town. And while we're at it let's send the Bruford Brothers a telegram asking them if they can furnish us with the serial numbers of the Kansas City bank notes Simpson was carrying."

I guess I'd better explain about paper money back in those days. Each bank issued its own bank notes which were redeemable in gold at that particular bank. It wasn't until 1913 when the Federal Reserve System was established that the Government of the United States started printing its own paper money and banks stopped issuing their own bank notes. Most of the bank notes in Adenville were on Utah banks.

I figured for sure Tom's great brain had failed him when we entered the marshal's office the next day after school. Both Uncle Mark and Sheriff Baker really looked down in the dumps.

"I was wrong?" Tom asked as if he'd just lost the ball game.

"No," Uncle Mark replied. "You were dead right. We found out Fred Pearson hasn't changed his mind about making good his nephew's gambling debts. He thinks Hutch has got a lucky streak going for him at the Fairplay Saloon."

Tom got a puzzled look on his freckled face. "But doesn't that mean the money Hutch is losing came from the train robbery?" he asked.

"No doubt about it," Uncle Mark said. "Bob Daniels, the proprietor of the Fairplay Saloon, told us that Hutch has lost over two hundred dollars. He still had the money in his safe and it was all in Kansas City bank notes. We've got leads on the whole gang. Sam Ludell is sweet on a dance hall girl named Rose at the Fairplay Saloon. He bought her several expensive dresses at Pearl Addison's Dress Shop and paid for them with Kansas City bank notes."

Tom nodded. "No wonder he tried to put the blame on Cassidy and the Wild Bunch."

"That ties Ludell in on it all right," Uncle Mark said. "And Herb Grant bought a new saddle from Jerry Stout's place paying for it with Kansas City bank notes. Curly Davis, a cowboy Pearson fired a couple of weeks ago, has lost more than a hundred dollars playing poker at the Whitehorse Saloon, all of it in Kansas City bank notes. Earl Eggerson who runs the dice table at the Fairplay Saloon bought an expensive watch and gold chain at the jewelry store with Kansas City bank notes. The sheriff and I are convinced that Hutch, Grant, Davis, and Eggerson held up the train and that Ludell was in on it."

Tom stared at the three empty cells. "Then why didn't you arrest them?" he asked.

Sheriff Baker cleared his throat. "Because District Attorney Vickers told us that he can't convict the men just because they are spending Kansas City bank notes," he said.

No wonder Uncle Mark and Sheriff Baker looked so down in the dumps.

Tom was shaking his head. "But don't they have to

prove where they got the money?" he asked the sheriff.

"The law doesn't work that way," Sheriff Baker said. "To get a conviction we would have to have the serial numbers of the bank notes Simpson was carrying in his money belt. We got an answer to the telegram we sent to the Bruford Brothers. They don't keep a record of the serial numbers themselves. But they did say it has been company policy for the cattle buyers themselves to keep a list of serial numbers since two of them were robbed. But . . ." he didn't finish the sentence, just shrugged helplessly.

"But what?" Tom asked.

"Your uncle removed all personal effects from the clothing Simpson was wearing before the body was shipped to Kansas City," Sheriff Baker said. "He did not find any list. After receiving the telegram your uncle and I searched Simpson's satchel and suitcase which we are holding for Mr. Perkins to take back to Kansas City. We didn't find any list of serial numbers."

"Then what happened to it?" Tom asked.

"My guess is that Simpson just forgot to make out a list of the serial numbers," Sheriff Baker said.

Just then Papa came into the office holding a telegram and looking excited. "I sent a copy of the *Advocate* with the story of the train robbery and murder to the editor of the *Hanksville Bugle,*" he said. "I knew Cassidy and his gang make Hanksville a sort of second home and thought the editor would be interested in knowing Cassidy had been identified as the man who killed Simpson. I just received this telegram from the editor. He wired me that Cassidy was seen in Hanksville the day of the train robbery by several people including himself."

Papa handed the telegram to Sheriff Baker who read it

and then handed it to Uncle Mark to read.

"This," Uncle Mark said, "makes a liar out of Sam Ludell. I think our best bet is to arrest Ludell and see if we can't get a confession out of him on the strength of this telegram and him spending Kansas City bank notes."

Sheriff Baker shook his head. "Ludell is a cool customer," he said. "He has to be or he couldn't be a blackjack dealer. He can always say the outlaw looked like Cassidy. And the bank notes mean nothing without the serial numbers."

"We have no choice," Uncle Mark said. "We've got to arrest Ludell before Saturday. Perkins will be in town buying cattle, and Adenville will be flooded with Kansas City bank notes by Saturday night."

Tom had been sitting with wrinkles in his forehead and concentrating with his great brain so hard that he wasn't even listening. Papa stared at him.

"What's on your mind, T.D.?" he asked.

Tom didn't answer. Just sat there. I nudged him with my elbow.

"Papa asked you a question," I said.

Tom blinked his eyes and then looked at our father. "I'm sorry, Papa," he said. "I was thinking."

"I know that look on your face," Papa said. "What were you thinking?"

Tom looked at Sheriff Baker. "Let Papa read that telegram from the Bruford Brothers about their cattle buyers keeping a list of serial numbers," he said.

Tom waited until Papa had read the telegram. "What kind of a man was Mr. Simpson?" he asked. "I mean was he a conscientious kind of man?"

"I've known Paul Simpson for about a dozen years,"

Papa said. "I would say he was a very conscientious man. Why do you ask?"

"Because if Mr. Simpson was a conscientious man," Tom said, "and knew it was company policy to keep a list of the serial numbers of bank notes he was carrying, then he must have made a list. Maybe he didn't want to carry the list on his person in case robbers searched him. Maybe he didn't want to put the list in his satchel or suitcase in case robbers took them believing he might have more money in them. My great brain has figured out there was only one way Mr. Simpson could make sure nobody but him ever got that list of serial numbers."

Uncle Mark and Sheriff Baker came up from their chairs as we stared at Tom.

Tom stood up. "The only way Mr. Simpson could make sure," Tom said, "was to mail the list to himself at the Sheepmen's Hotel. Did you ask if there was any mail for him at the hotel?"

Sheriff Baker slapped his hand on his hip. "No, we didn't," he said, "but by cracky we will now."

I don't believe Uncle Mark, Sheriff Baker, and Papa ever walked so fast in their lives. Tom and I had to run to keep up with them all the way to the hotel. Mr. Ricker was behind the desk. He had the longest neck and biggest Adam's apple of anybody in town.

Sheriff Baker spoke to him. "Are you holding any mail for Paul Simpson?" he asked.

Mr. Ricker's Adam's apple bobbed up and down as he talked. "I have a letter addressed to him in a Bruford Brothers envelope," he said. "Figured it must be company business, so I decided to hold it and give it to Mr. Perkins when he arrives Saturday."

ADENVILLE WEEKLY
Advocate
GREAT

"Give me the letter," Sheriff Baker ordered.

Mr. Ricker removed the letter from a box and handed it to the sheriff, who opened it. Sheriff Baker was grinning as he looked at the letter and then showed it to us. Across the top was written, "ADENVILLE, UTAH, TRIP BANK NOTE SERIAL NUMBERS," and below were listed the serial numbers.

Sheriff Baker patted Tom on the shoulder. "Thanks to your great brain we've got these outlaws cold," he said. Then he spoke to Uncle Mark. "We'll get Calvin Whitlock to open the bank so we can check the serial numbers of the Kansas City bank notes the gang has spent. And if they match any of the serial numbers written here, which I'm sure they will, we will arrest Hutch, Grant, Davis, Eggerson, and Ludell."

Papa said it was time for Tom and me to go home and do the evening chores. Then he added, "I'll be home late. Tell your mother to go ahead and have supper."

Tom and I started for home. "Boy, oh, boy," I said, "what a rotten deal. Your great brain solved the train robbery and murder and you can't be in on the most exciting part."

"It wouldn't look right," Tom said. "The outlaws know Sheriff Baker is a bachelor and that we aren't Uncle Mark's kids. They would wonder why the sheriff and marshal would let Papa bring along a couple of his kids."

But I couldn't help noticing that Tom was just as nervous as I was until Papa finally came home a little after seven o'clock and told us what had happened.

Uncle Mark and Sheriff Baker arrested the five men with the help of three deputies. They found a money belt on Hutch with over a thousand dollars in it in Kansas City bank notes. Herb Grant was also wearing a money belt with his share of the notes. Earl Eggerson had his share hidden in the toes of a pair of boots in his room at the Sheepmen's Hotel. Curly Davis had a receipt on him for an envelope he had deposited in the Whitehorse Saloon safe containing Kansas City bank notes. They didn't find any of the stolen money in Ludell's possession or in his room. But when they searched the room of his girl, Rose, they found Ludell's share of the bank notes he hadn't spent. She admitted Ludell had given her the money to hold for him.

With Curly Davis and Sam Ludell locked up in one cell and Herb Grant and Earl Eggerson in another and Hutch in a cell by himself, Sheriff Baker began the questioning with District Attorney Vickers and Papa present along with Uncle Mark. First Sheriff Baker showed Ludell the telegram Papa had received from the editor of the *Hanksville Bugle*.

"This proves you lied," Sheriff Baker said.

Ludell just shrugged. "I didn't lie," he said. "The man looked like Butch Cassidy, and I honestly believed it was him. And you can't send a man to prison for that."

Then Sheriff Baker showed all the outlaws the telegram from the Bruford Brothers about their cattle buyers keeping records of the serial numbers of bank notes they carried. Sheriff Baker then showed them the list of serial numbers Mr. Simpson had mailed to himself at the hotel.

"We knew all we had to do was wait until the gang who held up the train started spending Kansas City bank notes," Sheriff Baker said. "The serial numbers you see checked off are from bank notes that Davis and Hutchinson lost playing poker in the two saloons, that Grant used to buy a saddle from Jerry Stout, that Eggerson used to buy a watch and chain, and that Ludell used to buy dresses for Rose at Pearl Addison's Dress Shop."

Sheriff Baker then walked in front of the cell Hutch was in. "We also know," he said, "that you killed Simpson. He recognized you from that scar above your right eyebrow which the bandanna mask didn't cover. And when he called you Hutch you knew he'd recognized you and you killed him."

Then the sheriff walked back to his desk and sat down. "We will start with the bank notes in the money belt Grant was wearing," he said to Uncle Mark. "The district attorney and Mr. Fitzgerald will witness the serial numbers I cross off as you call them out."

Uncle Mark opened Grant's money belt. He removed the bank notes and made a pile of them. Then he began calling off the serial numbers. Sheriff Baker would locate the serial number on the list and check it off, then nod his head for Uncle Mark to call off the next serial number. Uncle Mark had only called off ten serial numbers when Grant pushed his face between the bars of the cell.

"That's enough," he shouted. "You've got us cold. But I wouldn't have gone in on it if I'd known there was going to be any shooting."

Eggerson was the next to crack. "Me neither," he said. "Sam and Hutch planned the whole thing but promised there would be no shooting."

Ludell then grabbed the bars of his cell and pushed his face against two of the bars. "I admit Hutch and I planned it," he said. "But Hutch promised there would be no shooting. I couldn't believe my eyes when I saw him kill Simpson in cold blood. The man didn't reach for a gun or anything. I'll turn state's evidence."

After Ludell said that, Hutchinson knew the game was up. "I had to kill him," he said. "I forgot all about that damn scar. I saw Simpson staring at it, and when he called me Hutch I knew he'd recognized me." Then he backed up and slumped down on the bunk in his cell. "I didn't want to kill him but I had to."

Sheriff Baker looked at Curly Davis. "That leaves just you," he said.

Davis stared at the sheriff for a moment and then looked at District Attorney Vickers. "If I plead guilty will I get a lighter sentence?" he asked.

District Attorney Vickers thought for a moment and then spoke. "To save the state the expense of a trial," he said, "I am willing to let four of you plead guilty to armed robbery and Hutchinson plead guilty to second degree murder. If you stand trial we have enough evidence to convict four of you as accessories to murder and send you to prison for life and enough evidence to see Hutchinson hang."

All five of them said they would plead guilty and signed confessions. On Monday morning Judge Potter sentenced Eggerson, Grant, Davis, and Ludell to twenty years in prison and Hutchinson to life.

I thought Tom would be very disappointed when he found out the Bruford Brothers weren't going to give any reward. I guess they figured Sheriff Baker and Uncle Mark were just doing their duty. Instead, on the day he found out there would be no reward he was whistling as we did the evening chores.

"I don't know how you can be so cheerful," I said. "If I were in your shoes I'd be so mad I could chew up railroad rails and spit out spikes."

"Simmer down, J.D.," he said. "Before I put my great brain to work on the train robbery and murder I made sure I'd get a reward if I solved the crime."

"Well," I said, "the Bruford Brothers sure as heck aren't going to give you a reward according to Sheriff Baker and Uncle Mark."

"You are forgetting the railroad," Tom said grinning. "Remember me telling you after lunch last Tuesday that I was going to the depot to talk to Mr. Larson before going back to school?"

"You said you wanted to talk to him about the train robbery," I said.

"Right," Tom said.

"Right what?" I asked.

"Yeah," said Frankie, who had been listening. "Right what?"

"I asked Mr. Larson if the railroad paid any reward money for train robbers," Tom said. "He told me there was a standing reward of five hundred dollars for the arrest and conviction of train robbers. Sheriff Baker will get the reward because the train robbery took place in the county under his jurisdiction. And Sheriff Baker isn't the kind of a man who goes back on his word."

"So," I said, "that is why you made him promise you all the reward money if you solved the train robbery and murder."

"Right," Tom said with a grin so wide I thought it would split his face.

"What are you going to do with all that money?" I asked.

"Put it in the bank where it will draw interest," Tom said as he rubbed the palms of his hands together.

And, oh, how his money-loving heart must have been singing.

CHAPTER FIVE

Tom the Magician

IT WAS JUST A FEW DAYS after Tom had received the five-hundred dollar reward that the Chautauqua came to town. Once a year people like Mayor Whitlock, Bishop Aden, Reverend Holcomb, Papa, Mamma, and Mrs. Vinson believed the citizens of Adenville needed a little cultural entertainment. The money to pay for the Chautauqua was raised by selling tickets before it arrived. It was a way of guaranteeing there would be enough money to pay for the cultural entertainment. I always sort of figured this selling of tickets was almost like blackmail because anybody who refused to buy a ticket would be considered uncultured and an ignoramus.

About the only thing I enjoyed about a Chautauqua was

watching them put up the tent at the campground. I guess that made me uncultured. But let me tell you what a Chautauqua was like in those days and see if you don't agree with me. They always had a fellow who played a fiddle but not like anybody in town played one. They called it classical music, but all it ever sounded like to me was a fellow practicing the scales. And there was always a man or woman who recited poetry the likes of which had never been heard in Adenville. I doubt if three people in the audience understood what the poems were about. And they had singers. But did they sing good old songs like "My Old Kentucky Home" or "Sweet Adeline"? Heck, no. Papa said they sang arias from operas, which was enough to convince me that I'd never spend any money going to an opera. The singing was bad enough, but they made it worse by always singing in a foreign language. Then they would have a man or woman who read passages from classical literature. That was the silliest thing of all. It didn't make sense unless you knew the whole story and the only time that happened was when a man read some passages from *A Christmas Carol* by Dickens. But he spoiled it by reading some passage from a Greek play written hundreds of years ago next. Sometimes they would act out a scene from one of Shakespeare's plays. And sometimes a fellow would play solos on a cornet. I must admit there was one time they had Swiss bell ringers which I enjoyed. They had a lot of different sounding bells on a table, and by ringing them they could play a tune.

The Chautauqua we had this year was the worst yet for my money. But rather than let anybody know they didn't understand or appreciate the classical stuff, everybody applauded. There was one woman who must have scared every dog in town. I mentioned her to Tom as we sat on the corral fence with Frankie the next morning after doing our chores.

"My ears are still ringing from that big fat woman screaming at the Chautauqua last night," I said.

"She was a soprano," Tom said. "That is the highest pitch a human voice can have."

"Why anybody would pay money to hear a woman like that beats me," I said. "The next Chautauqua that comes to town I'm going to pretend I'm sick and can't go."

"You know, J.D.," Tom said, "you are right in a way. I doubt if any kid in town enjoyed the Chautauqua. But you've given me an idea. I'm going to put on a magic show because I'm getting a little short of cash."

Tom's saying he was getting short of cash was like a dog all alone in a butcher shop complaining there wasn't enough meat.

"What do you mean by a magic show?" I asked.

"Yeah, what?" Frankie said.

"When I was at the Academy last year Father Rodriguez took all of us students to the Salt Lake Theater twice," Tom said. "Once was for a vaudeville show. Two of the best acts were the Mental Marvel, a mind-reading act, and Murdock the Magician. My great brain figured out how the Mental Marvel and his assistant faked the mind-reading act. But the magic tricks Murdock the Magician performed stumped me."

"He wouldn't come to a small town like Adenville," I said.

"Of course not," Tom said. "But I told Father Rodriguez my great brain had to know everything. He let me buy a book on how to do magic tricks. I studied it and found out how Murdock the Magician did some of his tricks. How much would you pay to see a magic show?"

"I've never seen a magic show," I said, "so how would

I know how much I would pay?"

"I'll give you an example," Tom said as he took a handkerchief from his pocket. "What if I told you this wasn't a handkerchief but a hen that could lay eggs?"

"I'd say your great brain is as scrambled as scrambled eggs," I answered and laughed because I thought that was funny and so did Frankie.

But not Tom. "All I'm asking you," he said serious as he could be, "is if I could show you a trick like that and a few other magic tricks, how much would you pay to see a magic show?"

"I'd gladly pay a dime to see a handkerchief lay an egg," I said and laughed some more because I thought that was even funnier and so did Frankie.

Tom put the handkerchief back in his pocket. "A dime," he said. "If I could get fifty kids at ten cents each that would amount to five dollars. I'll put my great brain to work on it right away and start rehearsing for my magic act."

For the next two days after school Tom took his book on magic and some things he wouldn't let me see up to his loft in the barn. He said he had to rehearse his magic act.

Thursday after school Tom said he needed a large wooden box to use as a table for his magic act. Frankie and I went with him to the Z.C.M.I. store taking along Frankie's wagon. The full name of the store was Zion's Cooperative Mercantile Institution. There were stores like this, which were owned by the Mormon church, in all Utah towns and cities. Tom asked Mr. Harmon if he could have one of the big wooden shipping boxes in back of the store. Mr. Harmon told Tom to help himself.

Tom picked out a wooden box large enough to use as a

table. I helped him lift it on to Frankie's wagon. Then Tom picked up a cardboard box and tossed it inside the wooden one. When we got to the barn we laid the box upside down after Tom had removed the cardboard carton. Tom sent me to the house to get Frankie's set of crayons. By the time I returned he had cut two pieces of cardboard from the carton. He used them and a black crayon to make two signs which read:

SEE ADENVILLE'S FIRST MAGIC SHOW
SUNDAY 2:00 P.M. ★ FITZGERALD BARN
ADMISSION 10¢
SATISFACTION GUARANTEED
OR YOUR MONEY BACK

Tom got a hammer and some tacks from the tool shed. He tacked one of the signs near the door of our barn. Then we went to the post office where he tacked the other sign to a tree in front of the building.

"What's the idea?" I asked. "Every kid in town will know about the magic show without any signs."

"I got to thinking," Tom said. "There are plenty of grownups who have never seen a magic show in Adenville. Maybe some of them will come too."

Papa always stopped at the post office to get the mail from our box before coming home for supper. He must have seen the sign because he stared at Tom with a suspicious look when he entered the parlor.

"I saw the sign for your magic show," he said. "Don't tell me that you are backsliding and this is another of your great brain's schemes to swindle people."

Tom looked as if Papa had accused him of robbing the bank. "How can it be a swindle when I guarantee satisfaction or your money back?" he asked. "I know if I'd never seen a magic show that I'd gladly pay a dime to see one."

"A magic show, yes," Papa said. "But magic acts are performed by professional magicians."

"I may not be a professional," Tom said, "but with my great brain I can do some tricks as good as any professional. And if you don't believe me come and see for yourself."

Then Tom told Papa about Murdock the Magician and the book on magic tricks he had bought. Papa was so relieved to find out that Tom wasn't backsliding that he offered to help.

"You will need seats for the audience," he said. "I'll get Mr. Hoffman at the lumber yard to lend us some planks we can lay on bales of hay."

"Thanks, Papa," Tom said. "But I sure wish I had a high silk hat to use for one of my tricks."

"Your mother knows where my plug hat is," Papa said. "Tell her I said you could use it."

Tom should have charged admission to the barn on Saturday morning. Papa and Uncle Mark came into the corral with my uncle's team and wagon. They had a load of planks loaned to them by Mr. Hoffman. About twenty kids kept getting in their way as they laid the planks on bales of hay, but they finally had six rows of seats for the audience. While they were doing this Tom and I put up a curtain in front of the box table. We used a piece of clothes line and an old sheet Mamma had given my brother.

The next day Tom asked Mamma to serve Sunday dinner an hour early to give him time to get ready for the magic show. We were all finished eating by one o'clock.

"I've got to get my props ready now," Tom said as he

stood up to excuse himself from the table.

"Just a moment," Mamma said. "When I got your father's high silk hat out I noticed his evening cloak. During our honeymoon in Denver we saw a magician perform at a vaudeville show. He wore a full dress suit, a high silk hat, and an evening cloak. You'll find the cloak and hat in my clothes closet."

"Thanks, Mamma," Tom said.

Frankie and I went with Tom into Mamma's bedroom. He got the plug hat and the evening cloak that was black silk on the outside and lined with white silk on the inside. We went to the barn. Tom put the cloak and hat on the box table. Then he and I climbed up the rope ladder to his loft. He handed me a cigar box, an alarm clock, and a steel bar about two feet long and half an inch thick. He picked up a shoe box and then we climbed down the rope ladder.

Tom opened the shoe box and removed a candleholder with a candle in it, a half-open box of kitchen matches, a steel ring about an inch in diameter, and a red bandanna handkerchief, which he laid out on the box table. He took the shoe box and went back up to his loft. When he returned I asked him what was in the shoe box.

"You'll find out during the show," he said. "Now, J.D., I'm going to hire you to collect admissions, and remember no credit or promises. Keep the money in the cigar box."

"What am I supposed to do with the alarm clock?" I asked.

"You will need it to know what time it is," he answered. "I've got it all set. Don't open the barn doors until a quarter to two. At one minute to two you close the barn doors and bring the cigar box and alarm clock backstage."

"Where is backstage?" I asked.

"Behind the curtain," Tom said. "Then you step around in front of the curtain and say, 'I am proud to present Adenville's first magic show with that great conjurer, T.D. Fitzgerald.' "

"What's a conjurer?" I asked.

"Yeah, what?" Frankie said.

"A magician," Tom said as if disgusted.

"Then why don't I say magician?" I asked. "None of the kids will know what a conjurer is any more than I did."

"I can't help that," Tom said. "Conjurer sounds more mysterious."

"What do I get for collecting admissions and introducing you?" I asked because I wanted some guarantee before the show started.

"I'll pay you twenty-five cents," Tom answered.

"What if nobody comes?" I asked. "Will I still get the quarter?"

"If you are low-down enough to take it," Tom said. "Now get going."

I sure as heck didn't have to be low-down to take the quarter. By one thirty I was regretting that I hadn't driven a harder bargain. The show wasn't due to start until two o'clock but there were already about twenty kids in the corral. And by the time I opened the barn doors and began collecting admissions just about every boy in town was there, along with five girls and six adults. Tom was going to make a fortune.

Most of the customers had paid and were in the barn when I saw Papa, Mamma, Aunt Bertha, Aunt Cathie, and Uncle Mark come into the corral. Boy, oh, boy, what a spot that put me in. Should I charge our own family to see the show or let them in free? I knew if I let them in free what

Tom would say with his money-loving heart. He would say I should have charged them fifty cents. Then he would say that because I let them in free, instead of him owing me twenty-five cents, I owed him a quarter. Papa solved my problem by handing me fifty cents.

I waited until one minute to two and then entered the barn and shut the door. I went "backstage" as Tom called it. He was peeking through a hole he had cut in the sheet curtain. He turned and looked at me the way a hungry horse would look at a manger full of oats.

"We are playing to a full house," he said grinning. "The seats are all filled and there are even some adults standing up. How do I look?"

He had on Papa's evening cloak and high silk hat, which was pressing down on his ears.

"I don't know if you look like a magician or not," I said, "because I've never seen one."

Tom took the cigar box and alarm clock from me and placed them behind the box table. "All right, J.D.," he said, "make your announcement and then draw the curtain."

I stepped around in front of the curtain. "I am proud to present Adenville's first magic show," I said, "with that great conjurer, T.D. Fitzgerald." Then I couldn't help adding, "For the benefit of you kids who don't know what a conjurer is, it is the same as a magician."

I didn't see anything funny about it, but Papa and some of the other adults laughed. They all stopped laughing when I pulled the curtain over and revealed the great conjurer himself. Tom stood behind the box table wearing the high silk hat and evening cloak with his arms folded on his chest. Everybody in the audience began to applaud, and he hadn't even done anything yet.

"Ladies and gentlemen," Tom said when the applause died down, "is the hand quicker than the eye? Some people say Yes and some say No. Do conjurers have supernatural powers that enable them to perform feats of magic? Some people say Yes and some say No. Today I am going to let you decide the answers to these two questions yourself by performing three of the most difficult magic tricks known."

Tom removed the high silk hat and held it so the audience could see inside it. Then he laid it on the table. He removed the evening cloak and showed the audience the inside and outside before putting it back on.

"You have seen there is nothing in the hat," Tom said. "And you have seen there are no hidden pockets in the cloak." He then rolled the sleeves of his shirt up above his elbows and left them there. "You can also plainly see, ladies and gentlemen, that I have nothing up my sleeves." He held up his hands with fingers spread apart showing the back and palm of both hands. "And you can plainly see that I have nothing concealed in my hands. I will now proceed to do my first magic trick by turning the flame of a candle into a red handkerchief."

Tom picked up the half-open box of kitchen matches. He removed a match with his right hand and then closed the box. He put the box of matches on the box table and then lit the match on the side of it. He used the match to light the candle in the candleholder with his right hand. Then he held the doubled up fist of his left hand above the flame of the candle.

"Abracadabra, abracadabra," he chanted. "Flame of candle enter my fist and become a red handkerchief when I blow you out."

Tom blew out the candle. Then he held up his left fist.

He opened his fingers slightly. Then using his right thumb and index finger he drew a red handkerchief from his left fist. He waved it back and forth and then placed it on the table.

Everybody in the audience applauded except some kids who were so bug-eyed with astonishment they just sat there staring with their mouths open.

Tom put the candle and box of matches behind the box table. Then he held up the shoe box sideways.

"I know you are all wondering what I've got in this shoe box," he said. "I will tell you. I have a magic hen in this shoe box whose name is Henrietta."

The audience laughed.

"Please don't laugh," Tom said, very serious. "If you hurt Henrietta's feelings she might refuse to lay an egg for me."

The audience laughed some more.

Tom put the shoe box down. He picked up Papa's high silk hat and showed the audience the inside.

"As you can see the hat is empty," he said as he put it back down. "I will now get Henrietta to lay an egg in the hat."

He took the lid off the shoe box and stared inside. Then he faced the audience.

"Now look what you have done," he said. "You hurt Henrietta's feelings by laughing at her. I told you she was a magic hen. She has cast a spell over the audience so you will think you are seeing just a plain old white handkerchief instead of a hen."

Tom reached into the shoe box and held up a white handkerchief by two corners. "I know this looks like a white handkerchief to you," he said. "But I am actually holding

Henrietta in my hands. I will prove she is a real hen by making her lay an egg in the hat."

Tom placed the handkerchief over Papa's hat which was turned upside down. "All right, Henrietta," he said, "lay me an egg like a good hen."

Everybody started to laugh.

"Come on, Henrietta," Tom pleaded. "Please lay me an egg."

It was so comical, Tom's talking to a handkerchief as if it were a hen that understood English, everybody laughed some more.

"All right, Henrietta," Tom said looking angry, "if that is the way you want to be. You lay me an egg right now or I'll have my mother make a chicken stew out of you."

That made the audience roar with laughter.

Tom held up his hands for silence. "Quiet please," he said as he bent his head closer to the hat. "She's cackling and clucking now. She is going to lay me an egg. She did it!"

People in the audience were now laughing so hard some of them were holding their sides. But not for long. Tom peeled the handkerchief back holding it and the brim of the hat. He kept the hat in plain sight as he walked around in front of the box table. Then he tipped the hat so everybody in the audience could see inside. And lying in the hat was a white egg.

Tom walked in back of the box table. He put the hat down. He picked up the handkerchief by two corners and carefully put it back in the shoe box.

"Don't cry, Henrietta," he said. "I was just joking about making a chicken stew out of you."

The audience, which had been stunned into silence when they saw the egg inside the hat, now began to applaud and whistle. Tom put the lid on the shoe box and placed it behind the box table. He took several bows and then held up his hands for silence.

"I have saved the most difficult of all magic tricks for last," he said. "But this trick can't be done unless I'm wearing the magic hat." He picked up the hat.

"The egg!" I and about twenty other kids yelled at the same time.

Tom didn't pay any attention to us. He put the high silk hat on his head. I expected to see egg yolk running from under the hat and down Tom's face, and so did everybody else in the audience. There was a dead silence when nothing happened. Finally Danny Forester cupped his hands to his mouth and shouted from the rear of the audience.

"What happened to the egg?" he yelled.

Tom removed the plug hat and held it so the audience could see inside it. "What egg?" he asked, looking as innocent as he could be.

"The egg that was in the hat!" Danny shouted.

"Oh, that egg," Tom said. "I knew I had to use the magic hat for my next trick so I made it disappear."

That got almost as much applause as the original egg trick. Tom put the hat back on and picked up the steel bar and steel ring from the box table. He rapped the ring against the steel bar making a clinking sound. Then he motioned to me to take the steel bar.

"My assistant will now pass among the audience and allow you to examine the steel bar," he said. "I want you to make sure it is a solid piece of steel."

A dozen kids insisted on examining the steel bar and so did Seth Smith's father and Don Huddle the blacksmith. Tom used his handkerchief to blow his nose while this was going on. When I returned the steel bar to him he took hold of the end of it with his right hand and then handed me the steel ring with his left hand.

"My assistant will now pass among you," he said, "and let you examine the steel ring to make sure it is a solid steel ring."

While I was doing this Tom slid the steel bar so he was holding it with his right hand around the middle. Again Mr. Smith and Mr. Huddle examined the steel ring, along with about twenty kids. When I returned it to Tom he held it up with the thumb and index finger of his left hand.

"I will now ask for two volunteers from the audience," he said, "to help me perform the impossible. How about you, Basil, and you, Danny?"

Tom then came around from behind the box table holding the steel bar in one hand and the steel ring in the other hand. He told Danny to stand on one side of him and Basil on the other side.

"Now, Danny," he said, "pick up that red bandanna handkerchief on the table and drape it over my right hand holding the steel bar."

Tom waited until the bandanna had been placed over his right hand covering it from view. "Now, Danny," he said, "you take hold of one end of the steel bar with your right hand, and Basil, you take hold of the other end with your left hand."

Both boys took a firm grip on the steel bar. Tom held up the steel ring in his left hand.

"There is no way I can put the steel ring around the steel bar without using magic powers," he said.

Then he placed his left hand and the steel ring under

the red bandanna handkerchief. "Abracadabra, abracadabra," he chanted. "Using all my magic powers, I now command the steel bar to part in the middle so I can put the steel ring around it."

I think everybody in the audience held their breath as Tom stood staring at the red bandanna handkerchief.

"Abracadabra, abracadabra," Tom chanted. "I now command the steel bar to join itself together so nobody will ever know it parted to let me put the ring around it."

Again there was dead silence for a moment. "Abracadabra, abracadabra," Tom chanted. "I now command the steel ring to spin on the steel bar when I count to three and remove my hands and the bandanna handerkerchief. One, two, three!"

On the count of three Tom removed his hands jerking the bandanna handkerchief quickly away from the steel bar. I thought my own eyes and the eyes of everybody in the audience were going to pop right out of our heads. The steel ring was around the steel bar and spinning.

Tom laid the bandanna handkerchief down on the box table. Then he used his own handkerchief to wipe his forehead. For my money, his whole body should have been wringing wet with sweat after pulling a magic trick like that.

Danny and Basil were still holding the steel bar. Danny's left eyelid which was usually half closed was wide open, and so was his mouth. Basil kept blinking his eyes as he stared at the steel bar and steel ring as if he couldn't believe them. Finally Danny recovered enough to speak.

"I still don't believe it," he said.

"Examine the steel bar and ring all you want," Tom said.

Danny let go of the steel bar and removed the ring. He stared at the ring for a moment and then put it in his mouth and bit on it.

"Ouch!" he yelled.

Then Basil took the steel bar and tried to bend it but couldn't.

Mr. Smith and Mr. Huddle came up to the box table. They both examined the steel bar and steel ring and then walked back to their seats shaking their heads.

All of this time the audience had been silent with astonishment. Then somebody began to applaud, and everybody joined in.

Tom took several bows and then held up his hands for silence. "Thank you very much ladies and gentlemen," he said. "That concludes Adenville's first magic show. I can tell from your applause that all of you are satisfied you got your money's worth."

That was a clever thing for Tom to say. A kid who had been applauding and whistling would have to have a coconut for a head to say he wasn't satisfied and wanted his money back. But I could tell by how excited they looked as they left the barn that they were all more than satisfied. Tom waited until everybody had left except Frankie and me and then counted the money in the cigar box. He had five dollars and forty cents. He gave me the quarter he had promised. But all that money made me a little greedy I guess.

"That pays me for collecting admissions and introducing you," I said. "Now how about paying me for acting as your assistant? That ought to be worth another quarter."

"You've got cabbages in your head," Tom said. "By rights I should make you pay me for letting you be my assistant. There isn't a kid in town who wouldn't have jumped at the chance to be my assistant and get to see the show free."

I knew he was right. "That is a lot of money for putting on a magic show," I said. "But I'll bet the kids would pay even more to see how you did all those tricks."

"I thought about doing just that," Tom said. "But my great brain said No."

"Why?" I asked.

"Yeah, why?" Frankie said.

"If I showed the kids how the tricks were done," Tom said, "they would know they had been tricked by sleight of hand. And knowing they had been tricked, some soreheads among them would start yelling I'd swindled them and demand their money back. But as long as they think I performed the tricks by magic none of them can claim they were swindled."

"But you were just putting on a magic show," I said. "I'll bet none of the customers at the Salt Lake Theater claimed Murdock the Magician had swindled them and demanded their money back."

"Murdock the Magician and I are two different people," Tom said. "He is a professional magician. I'm a fellow who must watch his *P*'s and *Q*'s with everybody just waiting to catch me backsliding."

"How about showing just Frankie and me how you did the tricks if we promise never to tell?" I asked.

"And also us," Papa's voice made us all turn around. "We waited until everybody had left."

We hadn't heard Papa, Uncle Mark, Mr. Smith, and Mr. Huddle enter the barn.

"I'm sorry," Tom said as he hugged the cigar box with both hands, "but I can't."

"If you are worrying about me making you refund the

admission money forget it," Papa said. "You put on a good show, and it was worth every penny you charged to see it."

"In that case," Tom said, "I'll show you."

He put down the cigar box and picked up the box of kitchen matches and the candle in its holder from behind the box table. He set the candleholder down. Then he pushed the box of kitchen matches half open. He picked up the red handkerchief and rolled it up into a ball and placed it in the opposite end of the open box of matches.

"I never let the audience see this end of the box of matches where the red handkerchief is hidden," Tom said. "And after I removed a match with my right hand I pushed the matchbox closed which forced the rolled-up handkerchief into the palm of my left hand. I palmed the handkerchief in my left fist."

"I guessed that much," Papa said. "But the other two tricks baffled me."

Tom removed the high silk hat he was still wearing and placed it upside down on the box table. He got the shoe box and placed it sideways on the table. He removed the lid and lifted out the white handkerchief, holding it by two corners.

"I only let the audience see one side of the handkerchief," he said. Then he crossed his arms and turned the handkerchief around. "The audience never saw this side."

Up close I could see a piece of white thread sewn to the top hem of the handkerchief and an egg hanging just below the middle of the handkerchief on the other end of the thread.

"I know you are wondering about the egg," Tom said. "But it is just an empty shell. I used a needle to punch a hole in each end. Then by blowing softly on one end I was able to blow the contents inside the shell out the hole on the other end. Then I took some white glue and pasted the end of the thread to the top of the eggshell."

Tom turned the handkerchief around so we couldn't see the eggshell. Then he laid the handkerchief over the plug hat just as he had done before the audience.

"The trick is to lift up the handkerchief by the two corners opposite the ones I was holding when I put it over the hat," he explained. He took hold of the two opposite corners and lifted them up. "You can see that leaves the eggshell lying on the bottom of the hat. Then by holding the opposite end of the handkerchief from where the thread is sewn to the hem, and taking hold of the brim of the hat, I can show the eggshell in the hat to the audience. I know from that distance they can't see the white thread against the white silk lining inside the hat."

Tom placed the hat back on the table and covered it with the handkerchief. "Now the trick is when I pick up the handkerchief I take hold of the two corners where the thread is sewn to the hem." He took hold of the two corners and lifted up the handkerchief. "Holding it this way to put it back in the shoe box the audience can't see the eggshell on the opposite side."

Papa shook his head as Tom put the handkerchief and eggshell back in the shoe box. "Sounds simple when you know how it is done," he said. "Did you make up that dialogue about Henrietta? It was funny and clever."

"No," Tom admitted. "Some of it I remembered Murdock the Magician using. I just made up that part about letting Mamma make stewed chicken out of Henrietta."

Don Huddle picked up the steel bar from the table. "As a blacksmith who works with metal," he said, "I thought that last trick was the best of all. But I can't for the life of me figure out how you did it."

"It was easier than the egg trick," Tom said. "I got two identical bridle rings from Mr. Stout at his saddle and harness shop. While J.D. was letting the audience examine the steel bar I pretended to blow my nose."

Tom removed his handkerchief and blew his nose and then returned it to his pocket. He then showed us a steel ring he had palmed under the thumb of his right hand.

"That is how I got the duplicate ring into my right hand," he said. "When J.D. handed me the steel bar I slipped the duplicate ring over it while the audience was examining the other steel ring. Then I slid the ring to the middle of the bar covering it with my fist."

Mr. Huddle scratched his chin. "How did you get rid of the other ring?" he asked.

"When I put my left hand under the bandanna handkerchief," Tom said, "I palmed the other ring. And when I drew my hands and the bandanna away from the steel bar, I laid the bandanna on the box table. Then I used my handkerchief to wipe sweat from my forehead and put the other ring in my pocket."

I had a question to ask. "How did you make the ring spin on the steel bar?"

"By jerking the bandanna handkerchief away quickly," Tom answered.

Mr. Huddle shook his head. "You had me completely buffaloed on that one, Tom," he said. "Thanks for showing me how it was done. I wouldn't have been able to sleep nights trying to figure it out."

"You haven't seen anything yet," Tom said. "In my next magic show I'm going to saw J.D. in half."

"Oh, no, you aren't," Papa said. "We will leave the sawing of people in half to the professional magicians. I don't want you practicing any dangerous tricks with your brother. And just to make sure you don't, I think you should leave well enough alone and forget about any more magic shows. We will all keep your confidence and not reveal how you did the magic tricks today. But this is the end of your career as a magician. Is that understood?"

"Yes, Papa," Tom said.

I didn't blame Tom for looking plumb disgusted as Papa, Mr. Smith, Mr. Huddle, and Uncle Mark left the barn.

"Papa is such a worry wart at times," he said. "I saw Murdock the Magician saw a woman in half. It is just an illusion and it tells how to do it in my magic book."

"Put me down as a worry wart too," I said. "The day I let you practice sawing me in half I'll have onions growing out of my head instead of hair."

"But I told you it is just an illusion," Tom said.

"I don't care what you call it," I said. "I'm not a fellow who is going to take a chance of having his hips and legs running around this barn looking for the rest of his body because the trick doesn't work."

Frankie began laughing. "That would be funny," he said.

"You call that funny?" I asked.

"Yeah," Frankie said. Then he bent over and began running around inside the barn yelling, "Where's the rest of my body?"

That made Tom and me both laugh.

The fellows began pestering Tom so much wanting to know how he did the magic tricks, he had to tell them a lie to stop it. He said Murdock the Magician had taught him magic and he had promised never to reveal how it is done.

CHAPTER SIX

Puppy Love

REPORT CARDS CAME OUT once a month. We received our first, for the month of September, a few days after Tom had put on his magic show. As expected, The Great Brain got all *A*'s. I got one *A* and only one *C* and the rest were *B*'s, which was darn good for a fellow with a little brain. Frankie got good marks in everything.

The day after we received our report cards Tom, Frankie, and I did our homework on the dining room table. Then we went into the parlor. Papa looked up from the weekly mail edition of the *New York World* he was reading.

"How is your teacher coming along, T.D.?" he asked.

"Mr. Monroe is doing just fine." Tom said. "Since he

got over his nervousness those first few days, he is a good teacher."

"Nels Larson doesn't think so," Papa said. "Knowing I am on the board of directors for the Academy, he dropped in at the *Advocate* office today. He told me he was very disappointed that his son Greg got such low marks on his report card. Greg attended a Mormon boarding school in Provo last year for the seventh grade. His grades were excellent. Mr. Larson said his son blamed the poor marks he got at the Academy this first month on Mr. Monroe's being a poor teacher."

"That is a big fib," Tom said. "Sally Anne Carver is responsible for Greg's poor grades."

Mamma dropped her crocheting into her lap. "What has Sally Anne Carver got to do with Greg Larson's poor grades?" she asked.

"He doesn't pay attention in class," Tom said. "All he does is sit and stare at Sally Anne. She has got poor Greg completely hypnotized with her giggling."

"Surely," Mamma said, "Mr. Monroe doesn't permit giggling in school."

"Of course not," Tom said. "But every time Greg goes by her home she runs to the front gate and swings on it and giggles. And she giggles at him during recess and every time she sees him. My great brain figured out a long time ago that giggling is how a girl puts a spell on a fellow."

I don't know why, but that made Mamma, Papa, and Aunt Bertha laugh. Every time a girl looked at me and started giggling I stuck my fingers in my ears.

"It isn't funny," Tom said. "Greg wants to be a railroad stationmaster like his father. But if he fails in school he won't be able to go away to high school next year. Next thing you know poor old Greg will be so hynotized he'll be going over to sit on the front porch swing with Sally Anne."

"You are right," Papa said. "Puppy love isn't funny. It can be a very serious thing in a boy's or girl's life. I remember my first case of puppy love when I was about Greg's age. Her name was Agnes Murphy."

Mamma stared at Papa. "And just who was Agnes Murphy?" she asked, rather sharply I thought.

"I was only fourteen at the time," Papa protested.

"Answer the question," Mamma said.

"I thought she was the prettiest girl in Boylestown, Pennsylvania," Papa said smiling. "I do believe you are jealous, Tena."

"I'm jealous of every girl you ever knew," Mamma said, but she was smiling when she said it.

Tom folded his arms on his chest. "How do you break a spell a girl puts on a boy with her giggling?" he asked.

I was dumbfounded. It was one of the very few times I'd ever heard Tom admit that his great brain didn't know everything.

"Puppy love is just something you outgrow," Papa said.

"Well, Greg better outgrow it pretty darn soon," Tom said, "or he is going to fail in school. I guess I'll have to put my great brain to work on how to break the spell before that happens. I like Greg."

One thing I could never figure out was what girls were good for. Today boys and girls play together, and girls play all the games boys do. But back in those days things were different. It was a disgrace for a boy to have anything to do with a girl until he was sixteen or he was called a sissy. And girls didn't play any of the games boys did like baseball, football, leapfrog, or kick-the-can. All they did was play hopscotch and jacks, play house, play with dolls, skip rope, and things like that.

Sweyn had disgraced Tom, Frankie, and me by starting to go with Marie Vinson after his first year at the Jesuit Academy when he was only thirteen. He had to whip three boys for calling him a sissy. Nobody called him a sissy after that, but that didn't stop the shame and disgrace I felt. The only time us boys had anything to do with girls was at birthday parties. We had to go to theirs and invite them to ours because our parents made us.

What Greg saw in Sally Anne Carver was a mystery to me. She was just a girl. Being a fellow who prided himself on never having anything to do with girls I didn't know if she was pretty or not. I'll admit she wasn't knock-kneed, bowlegged, or pigeon-toed, which I guess was in her favor. But she was just a silly girl like all the rest. I felt sorry for Mr. Carver because he had three daughters and no sons. With nothing but females running around the house Mr. Carver would have been driven to drink if he weren't a Mormon. Their religion forbids them to drink any kind of alcoholic beverage.

And I couldn't figure out why any girl would want to put a spell on a fellow like Greg. He had buckteeth that hung over his lower lip. His blond hair grew forward instead of backward, coming down over his eyes like a sheep dog's. Poor old Greg. Only Tom's great brain could save him from a fate worse than drink or death.

The following Saturday morning I started for Smith's vacant lot with Tom and Frankie to play. The Carver home was on Main Street just two blocks from our house. When we arrived at the corner we all stopped and stood staring bug-eyed. Greg was showing off on his bike in front of the

Carver home. Sally Anne was swinging on the front gate watching him and giggling. Greg rode by the house without using the handlebars on the bike.

Tom motioned for me and Frankie to follow him down a side street. "My great brain has a plan to save Greg," he said. "Come on."

We ran all the way to Smith's vacant lot where Tom gathered the fellows around him.

"Sally Anne has got poor old Greg completely hypnotized," Tom told the fellows. "She's got him so much under her spell that he is failing in school. It is up to us to save him."

Danny's left eye lid flipped open. "And how do we do that?" he asked.

"My great brain has figured out a way to break the spell," Tom said. "Greg is showing off on his bike in front of her house right now. We go there and when I give the signal we all run into the street and begin shouting, 'Greg's got a girl,' over and over again. That should make him so ashamed and humiliated it will break the spell."

We all followed Tom at a run to the side street leading off Main Street. Tom peeked around the corner.

"Greg is at the other end of the block turning around," Tom said. "When he starts back and gets in front of Sally Anne's house we will all run out and start shouting. Get ready. Here he comes. Now, fellows!"

Greg was riding his bike standing with one foot on the seat, his other leg stuck out behind him over the rear wheel, and his body bent over his hands on the handlebars as we ran into the street.

We all began to shout as we ran towards him, "Greg's got a girl," over and over again. He was so surprised that he fell off his bike. We formed a circle around him and continued to shout, "Greg's got a girl!"

He was so ashamed and humiliated his face was the color of red-hot coals. You would think a girl with any pity would have run into the house. But not Sally Anne. She just stood by the front gate giggling as if she enjoyed Greg's humiliation. I thought for sure Greg would pick up his bike and get as far away from Sally Anne as possible. Instead he picked up the bike and wheeled it over and leaned it against the Carvers' front fence. And I'll be a six-legged mule if he didn't walk up to Sally Anne and begin talking to her. We all stopped shouting and looked at Tom. Parley Benson pushed his coonskin cap to the back of his head.

"Your great brain's plan only made it worse," he said.

"She is keeping him under her spell with her giggling," Tom said.

Danny shook his head. "Then your great brain better figure out a way to stop Sally Anne from giggling," he said.

And then came positive proof that a girl can hypnotize a fellow with her giggling. Sally Anne opened the gate. She put her hand in the crook of Greg's elbow and the two of them began walking down Main Street bold as brass. We were all as surprised as a hen who hatches a turkey egg. Parley was first to speak.

"I wonder where they are going," he said.

"Only one way to find out," Tom said.

We followed Greg and Sally Anne to the drugstore where we pressed our faces against the window to watch. Sammy Leeds was working behind the soda fountain. He stared at Greg and Sally Anne as if they were two dogs who had sat down at the counter and asked to be served. He kept blinking his eyes as if he couldn't believe what he was seeing as he prepared two chocolate ice cream sodas and placed them on the counter.

Parley shook his head. "He's a gonner for sure," he said.

Did Tom give up? Heck, no.

"Maybe my great brain can save him yet," he said.

Danny rammed a finger into Tom's chest. "Your great brain has made the spell ten times worse," he said. "When a boy starts buying ice cream sodas for a girl there ain't anything that can break the spell."

We waited until Greg and Sally Anne came out of the drugstore. We followed them to the Carver home. Greg said good-bye to Sally Anne. Then he got on his bike and rode to Smith's vacant lot with us running to keep up with him. He got off his bike and drew a line in the dirt with the toe of his shoe. He spit on the palms of his hands and then doubled up both fists.

"All right," he said. "Who's first?"

Tom put his arm around Greg's shoulders. "Nobody is going to call you a sissy," he said sympathetically. "We know it isn't your fault that Sally Anne has you hypnotized with her giggling. We were just trying to break the spell."

"Maybe she has got me under her spell," Greg said, "but I like it. I asked her to be my girl and she said she would. You fellows don't know what you're missing."

Parley spat with disgust. "Missing what?" he asked. "You can't play boys' games with girls. You can't go fishing and hunting with them. All you can do is spend money buying them ice cream sodas and candy. What's the good of having a girl?"

"It is hard to explain," Greg said. "I felt the same way you fellows do until I started having daydreams about Sally Anne."

"Boy!" Tom exclaimed. "She's really got you hypnotized. What kind of daydreams?"

"Like rescuing her from renegade Indians who were going to burn her at the stake," Greg said with a dopey, dreamy look on his face. "Like saving her from the railroad tracks where the villian had tied her just in the nick of time before the train came. Like saving her from having to marry the villain by paying off the mortgage."

Parley shook his head. "You've gone plumb loco," he said.

Greg became angry. "Do you want to back up those words with your fists?" he demanded.

"I'm not afraid to fight you," Parley said. "But I don't fight fellows who are plumb loco. I'll leave it up to the fellows. All of you who think Greg is nutty as a fruitcake hold up your hands."

We all held up our hands except Tom.

"What more proof do you want?" Parley asked.

"I don't care what you fellows think," Greg said. "Some day you will look at a girl and what happened to me will happen to you."

He walked over and picked up his bike.

"Just a minute," Tom said. "My great brain has figured out that girls put a spell on fellows with their giggling. Will you try an experiment and stuff cotton in your ears when you're near Sally Anne so you can't hear her giggling?"

"I will not," Greg said. "And what's more I'm calling on Sally Anne tomorrow night to sit on the front porch swing with her."

We all crowded around Tom after Greg left. Danny was the first to speak.

"I guess you haven't got such a great brain after all," he

said. "It only made things worse. Why didn't you use your fists instead of your brain? Why didn't you call Greg a sissy and fight him? You know darn well you can whip him. And maybe if you beat him up good it would have knocked some sense into him and broken the spell."

"I thought about it," Tom said. "But I didn't want to fight him for the same reason Parley didn't. Well, not exactly. Greg isn't insane. But he is bewitched, which is just as bad."

"Well," Danny said, "you had better put your great brain to work on how to save Greg. Tomorrow night he will be sitting on the front porch swing with Sally Anne. At the rate he is going he'll be married and have kids before he is old enough to shave."

Parley had a puzzled look on his face. "What do a boy and girl do when they sit on a front porch swing?" he asked.

"How should I know?" Tom asked.

"I thought your great brain knew everything," Parley said. "And besides I saw your brother Sweyn sitting on the front porch swing with Marie Vinson before he went away to school."

"I never asked Sweyn what he did," Tom said. "But you've given me an idea. I'll find out tomorrow night what Greg and Sally Anne do sitting on a front porch swing. Maybe that will give me a clue on how to break the spell."

Frankie and I had to go to bed at eight o'clock. Tom was twelve and allowed to stay up until nine o'clock. But Sunday evening he told Papa and Mamma he felt tired and went upstairs with Frankie and me.

"What's the idea?" I asked him as we entered our bedroom.

"Forget already?" Tom asked.

"Forget what?" I asked.

"Yeah, what?" Frankie said.

"I promised the fellows I'd find out what Greg and Sally Anne did on a front porch swing," Tom said.

I watched him take the screen off our bedroom window. "I'm going too," I said.

"Why?" Tom asked.

"Maybe you'll need a witness," I said.

"All right," Tom said. "Frankie, you go to bed. If it isn't too awful for a boy your age to hear we will tell you about it when we get back."

Tom and I climbed down the elm tree by our bedroom window. Our dogs Brownie and Prince came running to greet us. We locked them up in the barn so they couldn't follow us. We went down the alley until we were in back of the Carver home. They didn't have a dog so it was safe to enter the backyard. We walked around to the side of the house the porch swing was on. Then we got down on our hands and knees and crawled to the side of the porch which was about two feet off the ground. I could hear the porch swing creaking. Tom lifted up his head to take a look and so did I. Greg was sitting on one end of the porch swing and Sally Anne at the other end.

I admit that I didn't know what a boy and girl did on a front porch swing, but I'd always imagined they did mushy things like holding hands, hugging, squeezing, and even kissing. But Greg and Sally Anne sure as heck couldn't do any of these things sitting three feet apart. All I heard for a long time was the creaking of the swing. I began to wonder if boys and girls just sat on porch swings without talking to each other. Finally Sally Anne spoke.

"Did you say something?" she asked.

"No," Greg answered. "Did you say something?"

"No," Sally Anne said. "I thought you said something."

"No," Greg said. "I didn't say anything."

I sure as heck couldn't understand why a boy and girl would want to sit on a front porch swing and ask each other if they said something when they knew darn well they didn't. A few minutes passed and then Greg really did say something.

"Know how to make one word out of a new door?" he asked.

"No," Sally Anne answered. "How do you make one word out of a new door?"

"You take the first *o* from door," Greg said, "and the *n* and *e* from new and what does that spell?"

"One," Sally Anne answered.

"Then you take the *w* left in new," Greg said, "and the *o* and *r* and *d* left in door. And what does that spell?"

"Word," Sally Anne said.

"And that is how you make one word out of a new door," Greg said.

"That is clever," Sally Anne said.

I heard Tom grunt with disgust. I didn't blame him. It just goes to prove how dumb girls are. I knew that riddle when I was Frankie's age. Again there was no sound except for the creaking of the porch swing. Then a neighbor's dog barked.

"Did you say something?" Sally Anne asked.

Again they went through that did you say something, no, I didn't say anything, did you say something, business. And I couldn't help thinking that only a girl would think a barking dog sounded like a human being. Nothing but silence then for what seemed a long time. Finally Greg spoke.

"Want to play a word game?" he asked.

"I'd love to," Sally Anne said.

"I learned it at school in Provo last year," Greg said. "I'll name a city or state in the United States. Then you have to name one that begins with the letter the one I name ends with. Ready? Arizona, a state."

"I see," Sally Anne said. "Now I have to name one that begins with the letter *A*. Alabama, a state."

"Arkansas, a state," Greg said. "Now you must start with the letter *s.*"

"San Francisco, a city in California," Sally Anne said.

"Ends with an *o,*" Greg said. "Oregon, a state."

"Ends with an *n,*" Sally Anne said. "Let me think. Oh. Nevada, a state."

"Another *a,*" Greg said. "I think I'll give you one back. Augusta, capital of Maine."

Sally Anne laughed. "And I'll return the favor," she said. "Atlanta, capital of Georgia."

"I'm running out of *a*'s," Greg said. "No, wait a second. "Albany, capital of New York."

There was silence for a moment.

"Give up?" Greg asked. "If you do that means you go down one point and can use the next letter of the alphabet which would be *z*. And if you fail on *z* that puts you down two points and you go back to the beginning of the alphabet and use *a.*"

"Begins with a *y,*" Sally said. "Wait just a minute. The Revolutionary War. Got it. Yorktown, Virginia."

"Begins with an *n,*" Greg said. "New Orleans, a city in Louisiana."

"Begins with an *s,*" Sally said. "Oh, Salt Lake City, the capital of Utah. Now let me see you find a city or state that begins with a *y.*"

I don't know if Greg found one or not. Tom touched me on the shoulder. We crawled backwards to the side of the house and then stood up and stretched our aching muscles.

"Boy, oh, boy," I said when we reached the alley where we could talk. "Why would any boy rather sit on a front porch swing doing that instead of staying home and playing checkers or dominoes or some other good game?"

"That, J.D.," Tom said, "is something even my great brain can't figure out."

"Then you didn't get any kind of a clue that could help you break the spell?" I asked.

"The only clue I got," Tom said, "is that Greg might fail all other subjects in school but he ought to get an *A* in geography."

The next morning Danny, Parley, Seth, and some other fellows were waiting in front of our house when we left for school. They crowded around Tom wanting to know what he found out.

"You won't believe this fellows," Tom said, "but it is the God's truth and J.D. is my witness. We sneaked over to Sally Anne's front porch last night to listen to her and Greg. First they kept asking each other if they said something when they knew darn well neither one of them had said anything."

Parley pushed his coonskin cap to the back of his head. "That's silly," he said.

"It gets sillier," Tom said. "Then Greg told a stale old riddle and Sally Anne didn't know the answer. At least she pretended not to know. Then they began playing a word game to practice up on their geography. They were still playing it when we left."

I'd never seen such disappointed looks on the fellows'

faces. I guess they had been expecting to hear about holding hands, and hugging, and squeezing, and even kissing like I had.

Danny asked, "Is that all?"

"That is all," Tom said. "The only conclusion my great brain can come to is that when a girl casts a spell on a fellow, it makes both of them plumb soft in the head. My father calls it puppy love. There is nothing my great brain can do to break the spell."

It was the first time Tom's great brain had failed him, which only goes to prove how powerful the giggling of a girl can be. It not only hypnotizes a fellow but makes him a girl's slave. Greg began carrying Sally Anne's books home from school and followed her around like a little puppy dog follows his master. I guess that is why they call it puppy love. The only good thing was that Greg began getting good grades.

I did learn one valuable lesson out of it all. Sweyn had been thirteen when Marie Vinson put a spell on him with her giggling. Greg was thirteen when Sally Anne put her spell on him with her giggling. When I became thirteen I would buy myself a pair of ear plugs. And every time I got near enough to a girl to hear her giggling I'd stick those ear plugs in my ears so I couldn't hear. I'd show them I wasn't hiding in the cellar when the brains were passed out. They would never get me under their spell with their giggling.

CHAPTER SEVEN

The Wheel of Fortune

TOM'S FAILURE TO BREAK the spell Sally had put on Greg gave the fellows an opportunity to start belittling his great brain. They never passed up a chance to rub salt in Tom's wounds over it. I knew that if they kept it up Tom would put his great brain to work on how to get even with them. And sure enough on Saturday afternoon it happened. We were taking a rest after playing basketball in the alley behind our coal and wood shed.

Danny Forester winked at some of the fellows so Tom couldn't see him doing it.

"I wonder what happened to Tom's great brain," he said. "He couldn't break Sally Anne's spell on poor Greg."

Seth Smith nodded. "Maybe his great brain just shriveled up and died," he said.

Parley pushed his coonskin cap to the back of his head. "Could be," he said. "But maybe he never had a great brain in the first place."

Tom was sitting right there listening. "All right, fellows," he said. "That is enough."

Danny's left eyelid flipped open. "Can't blame us for being curious," he said. "You've been bragging for years about your great brain. Then along comes a girl and makes a fool out of you and your great brain."

Seth snapped his fingers. "Which just goes to prove," he said, "that if anybody in Adenville has a great brain it is Sally Anne Carver."

Tom stood up. "See you later," he said. "I'm going up to my loft."

I watched Tom walk toward our barn. "Now you fellows have done it," I said. "Tom is going up to his loft to put his brain to work on how to get even with you with one of his swindles."

Danny shook his head. "No, he won't," he said, "because Tom knows if he pulls off just one crooked deal no kid in town will have anything to do with him."

We continued playing basketball until it was chore time. I called up to Tom to come down and help with the evening chores.

"Did your great brain figure out how to get even with the fellows?" I asked.

"Not yet," he said. "But it will. They will rue the day they made fun of my great brain."

Tom's great brain didn't come up with a plan until Monday afternoon after school. I had to fix a tire puncture on my bike. After I finished I used the hand pump to pump up the tire. Then I figured as long as I had the bike upside down on the seat and handlebars I might as well oil it. I oiled the sprocket, the chain, and both wheels. Then I spun the wheels around to lubricate them. Tom and Frankie were sitting on the back porch steps watching me.

"Got it!" Tom said as he suddenly jumped to his feet. "The wheel of fortune."

"What is that?" I asked.

"Yeah, what?" Frankie said.

"It is a wheel with numbers on it," Tom said, "and each number wins a prize. You weren't living with us then, Frankie, but J.D. remembers the year they let a carnival come here for the County Fair. One of the booths was the wheel of fortune."

"I remember," I said. "I also remember so many people complained the games were crooked, the county commissioners barred any more carnivals from the County Fairs. The only good thing about it was the merry-go-round."

"I'll need a wheel," Tom said as his face became thoughtful.

I finished oiling my bike. "Maybe you could use an old bike wheel," I said.

"No," Tom said. "It has to be made of wood." He snapped his fingers. "Got it! Mamma never uses that old spinning wheel of Grandma's in the attic."

I went into the house with him. Mamma was busy in the kitchen with Aunt Bertha.

"Mamma," Tom said, "can I have that old spinning wheel of Grandma's in the attic?"

Mamma looked up from some biscuit dough she was kneading. "What in the world do you want it for?" she asked.

"To make a wheel of fortune," Tom said. "You know, like the wheel of fortune they had at the carnival that time."

"I also know," Mamma said, "that your father, your uncle Mark, and the mayor decided all the games of chance at the carnival were fixed so nobody won any prizes most of the time, and when they did, it was something very cheap. That is why no carnival has been allowed here since."

"But my wheel of fortune will be different," Tom said. "Somebody will win a prize every time and the prize will be worth more than it costs to play."

Mamma wiped her hands on her apron and placed her hands on her hips. "Something tells me I should say no," she said, "although I will never use the spinning wheel."

"Sometimes I just don't understand grownups," Tom said shaking his head. "I saw you and Papa playing the wheel of fortune and other games at the carnival and having fun even knowing the games were crooked. Now I want to make an honest wheel of fortune that has a winner every time so the kids can have some fun and you don't want to help me."

"I didn't say you couldn't have the spinning wheel," Mamma said. "And I guess there is no harm in you and your friends playing carnival. You can have the spinning wheel. Just make certain somebody wins a prize every time and there isn't any backsliding attached to it."

Tom and I got the spinning wheel from the attic and carried it to the barn with Frankie following us. Tom got some tools from the tool shed and took the spinning wheel apart. He told Frankie and me to throw everything but the wheel in the trash barrel.

While Frankie and I carried the extra parts to our trash

barrel Tom went up to his loft. He had a cigar box with several thread spools in it when he came down the rope ladder. Mamma always gave us the wooden spools after using the thread on them. A fellow could make a lot of things with a wooden spool, like a peashooter. Tom picked out a spool. He put a sixteen-penny nail through the hole. Then he hammered the nail into a wall joist in back of the box he'd used for a table during his magic act.

"The spool should hold the wheel far enough away from the two-by-four so it will spin," he said.

I watched him pick up the wheel and put the hub over the nail. He gave the wheel a spin and it went around and around.

"Now I need one of Papa's old celluloid collars," he said. "J.D., go ask Mamma if she's got one old and frayed enough to throw away."

Mamma said she was glad I'd reminded her because she had been meaning to buy some new celluloid collars for Papa. She picked out a worn one from the collar box and gave it to me.

Tom had the wheel lying on the box table when I returned. He was using a ruler and a pencil to make ten dots around the wooden rim of the wheel. When he finished he drove ten small nails into the rim where he'd made the dots. He put the wheel on the sixteen-penny nail.

Then he went to the coal and wood shed and picked out a stick about two inches wide and six inches long. Back in the barn he cut a strip of celluloid from the collar. He tacked one end of it to one end of the stick. This left about two inches of the celluloid below the stick. Tom placed the stick against the side of the wall joist above the wheel. The celluloid stuck out too far. He measured it with his eye and then cut off a piece of the stick. It fit perfectly then so he nailed the stick to the side of the wall joist. The piece of celluloid hung about a quarter of an inch below the nails on the wheel. Tom gave the wheel a spin. The celluloid made a clicking sound as it hit the nails while the wheel was spinning around and around.

"That is enough for today," Tom said. "It is time to start doing the chores."

The next day after school Tom used a board a foot wide and about six feet long to make a shelf on the barn wall beside the wheel.

"What is that for?" I asked.

"Yeah, what?" Frankie said.

"To display the prizes you can win playing the wheel of fortune," Tom said.

He went up to his loft and came back down with a calendar.

"Go to the house," he said to me, "and get a pair of scissors and some glue."

When I returned he took one month from the calendar and cut out the numbers one through ten. He glued them to the shelf about six inches apart. Then he cut out numbers one through ten from another month in the calendar. These he glued in the spaces between the nails on the wheel.

"All I need now," he said, "are some prizes and I'll be in business."

"When are you going to open for business?" I asked.

"Saturday morning at ten o'clock," Tom said. "But wait until Friday. Then you tell all the kids at the common school they are invited to play the wheel of fortune in our barn

Saturday morning. And make sure you tell them if they want to play to bring some money with them. I'll tell the fellows at the Academy."

Friday at noon Tom stopped at the bank on our way home for lunch. He exchanged three dollars for nickels.

"I'll need them to make change," he told Frankie and me. "It is going to cost a nickel to play the wheel of fortune."

When school let out that afternoon we went home and had cookies and milk. Then we went up to the bedroom to change into our play clothes. Tom got his bank from the clothes closet and took some money from it.

"I'm going to the Z.C.M.I. store to buy the prizes for the wheel of fortune," he said.

"Can I come?" I asked.

"No," Tom said. "I want you to do something. There are a lot of kids who graduated from the sixth grade who aren't going to the Academy. You know them. Take your bike and ride around and let them know about the wheel of fortune."

"It seems as if I'm doing a lot of work around here for nothing," I said. "What do I get out of all of this?"

"How about five cents?" Tom asked. "And that includes keeping the kids out of the barn tomorrow morning until I'm ready."

"Make it a dime," I said.

"All right," he said handing me a dime.

I was kicking myself as I rode around letting kids know about the wheel of fortune. Tom had given me the dime so quickly I knew I could have got a quarter just by asking. It was time to start doing the chores when I returned. Tom and Frankie were waiting on the back porch steps.

"It sure took you a long time," Tom said as he stood up.

"There are a heck of a lot of kids," I said, "whose parents believe a sixth grade education is all they need. Can I see the prizes?"

"You can see them tomorrow," Tom said.

The next morning we finished our chores in a hurry and just in time. The wheel of fortune wasn't supposed to start until ten o'clock, but kids started coming into the corral at nine thirty. Tom went inside the barn after telling me not to let anybody in until he called out to me. The fellows kept asking me what the wheel of fortune was, but Tom had told me not to tell them.

"You'll see for yourselves in a few minutes," I answered.

It seemed like more than half an hour before Tom called for me to open the barn doors. There were about twenty-five kids waiting by then. Tom was standing behind the box table by the wheel of fortune. He gave the wheel a spin.

"Behold the wheel of fortune," he said. "You will notice there is a number between each space on the wheel. Now, let me show you what prizes you can win if the wheel stops on the lucky number you hold."

He walked over to the shelf where the prizes were displayed. "There are ten numbers on the wheel of fortune," he said, "and ten numbers on the shelf. Behind each number on the shelf is the prize that number wins. For example, number one wins a genuine Spalding baseball worth thirty-five cents. Number three wins a harmonica worthy twenty-five cents. Number five wins a baseball mitt worth forty cents. Number seven wins a two-bladed pearl-handled pocket knife worth thirty-five cents. Number nine wins a bone-handled jackknife worth a quarter. And because there can be no losing numbers on a wheel of fortune, each of the other numbers wins two boxes of Cracker Jack worth ten cents with the usual prize in each box."

Tom walked in back of the box table and picked up some playing cards which he spread out like a fan.

"Now, this is how the game is played," he said. "I hold in my hand ten cards in the heart suit numbered from ace to ten. The ace counts as one. I shuffle the cards like this." He shuffled the cards. "Then I lay them face down on the box table like this." He placed the cards down one by one. "This way nobody knows what number he has until I spin the wheel of fortune. He might hold a number that can win a forty-cent prize. And again it might be a number that will only win a ten-cent prize. This makes it fair and square for everybody."

Parley thrust his head forward to look at the cards. "How much does it cost to play?" he asked.

"A mere five cents," Tom said, "to win a prize worth two times, five times, seven times, or even eight times that much. You place your nickel on top of one of the cards. As soon as I've collected the money, I will spin the wheel of fortune. Then you can look at your cards. All right, fellows, step right up and try your luck on the wheel of fortune."

So many kids started pushing and shoving each other to play Tom had to stop it.

"Take it easy," he said. "Line up and take your turn playing the wheel of fortune."

Danny, Parley, Seth, and the bigger kids got to play first. They each put a nickel on a card. Tom collected the money and put it in a cigar box. Then he spun the wheel of fortune.

"You can look at your cards now," he said. "And around and around she goes and where she stops nobody knows. Who will be the lucky winner? Only the wheel of fortune knows. It is slowing down now, slower and slower, and now it has stopped. The wheel of fortune says that number nine is the lucky winner."

Danny held up his card. "That's me!" he shouted.

"The prize for number nine is the bone-handled jack-knife," Tom said. "Now, you fellows understand that I only carry one of each prize so you can see what you win. So instead of giving Danny the knife, I'm going to give him twenty-five cents in cash so he can buy a knife just like it at the Z.C.M.I. store."

I had been wondering what Tom would do after somebody won a prize. I didn't have to wonder any longer. And I knew he hadn't gotten all those nickels at the bank just to make change. Did Danny leave the barn and go buy a jack-knife? Heck no. Tom knew that by giving cash instead of prizes most of the fellows would use the money to keep on playing instead of going to buy a prize like what they had won.

After paying Danny, Tom picked up the ten cards and shuffled them. He placed the cards face down on the box table.

"Let the next ten players step up and try their luck on the wheel of fortune," he said.

I got to play that time. I didn't win. My friend Howard Kay won two boxes of Cracker Jack. Tom gave him two nickels instead of the prize.

The kids kept on taking turns playing until lunch time. They won prizes with every spin of the wheel. But the only one who went down to the Z.C.M.I. store and bought a pearl-handled two-bladed knife with his prize money was Jimmie Peterson. The rest gambled the money right back. I lost the dime Tom had paid me plus fifteen cents on top of it and didn't win anything.

At noon Tom announced the wheel of fortune would close for lunch but would open again at one o'clock. He took the cigar box with him when we left the barn. He kept shaking it, as if the sound of clinking coins was music to his ears.

"You are making a fortune," I said as we walked toward the house with Frankie.

"Why not?" he asked grinning. "Every time I spin the wheel of fortune I have to make from ten cents to forty cents. And with five of the ten prizes just two boxes of Cracker Jack, it is forty cents half the time."

"This is the best swindle your great brain ever thought up," I said.

"If you think it is a swindle," Tom said, "you must be dumb as a billy goat."

For my money it was an out and out swindle. I couldn't see anything dumb about that.

"What do you mean?" I asked.

"Why did you play the wheel of fortune if you think it is a swindle?" Tom asked.

He had me there. And it was a good thing his mind was on the money in the cigar box or he would have blackmailed me into doing his share of the chores for saying it was a swindle.

Piggy banks sure took a beating during the noon hour. There were more kids playing the wheel of fortune that afternoon than there had been during the morning. Tom kept paying in cash instead of prizes, and the fellows all used the money to play some more. But with Tom keeping from ten cents to forty cents of the money bet each time, it wasn't too long before practically everybody was broke. By three thirty there were only five fellows left with any money.

"Sorry," Tom said, "but you can't play the wheel of fortune unless there are ten players."

It must have been Parley Benson's lucky day. He had won almost three dollars. Pete Kyle was also ahead of the game. Basil Kokovinis, Hal Evans, and Danny Forester still had some money left. Parley looked at Tom.

"There are five of us wanting to play," he said. "What if each of us pay a dime and take two cards?"

That was fine with Tom. But it only took a few spins of the wheel of fortune until Danny was broke. Parley was crazy for doing it, but to keep the game going he played four cards. A few more spins of the wheel and Hal was broke. Parley tried to get Basil and Pete to each play three cards but they refused. The game ended with Parley ahead a couple of dollars and Pete had won seventy cents, but everybody else had lost money.

I watched Tom count the money after the fellows left the barn. He was grinning when he finished.

"Except for Parley and Pete, I paid those fellows back good for making fun of my great brain," he said grinning. "I took them for fourteen dollars and thirty cents."

All that money made me feel a little envious. "You weren't running a wheel of fortune," I said. "You were running a gambling casino. And when Papa finds out you were giving cash instead of prizes he will make you give the money back."

Tom didn't look worried at all. "And just how is Papa going to find out?" he asked.

"Some of the fellows are sure going to complain to their parents that they were swindled," I said.

"Not one kid will dare to tell his parents," Tom said confidently.

"And why not?" I asked.

"Because they would have to admit they were gambling," Tom said. "And they all know their parents would give them a whipping for gambling."

Then I got a brilliant idea of how to get even with Tom for all the times he had blackmailed me.

"I know one kid who isn't afraid to tell his parents," I said. "You are looking at him. So maybe you'd better make me a partner and give me ten per cent of the profits."

"I see," Tom said. "Trying a little blackmail, eh, J.D.?"

"It takes one to know one," I said. "You never really reformed. You'll go on being a crook all of your life. And I can't see any harm in blackmailing a crook. Besides, it would make up for some of the times you blackmailed me."

Tom thought about it for a moment. "Now let me get this straight," he said. "You are going to tell Papa that I paid out cash instead of prizes if I don't make you a ten per cent partner. Right?"

"Right," I said.

"And I'm going to show Papa the prizes," Tom said, "and tell him my wheel of fortune was better than the one at the carnival because somebody won a prize every time. Papa would understand I couldn't have a dozen of each of the prizes on hand. Right?"

"I guess so," I had to admit.

"And because none of the fellows will dare tell their parents they were gambling," Tom said, "that means no parents are going to complain to Papa that I swindled their sons. Right?"

"Right," I was forced to admit.

"Therefore," Tom said, "when we tell Papa about the wheel of fortune, he is going to assume all the kids were satisfied and the winners went down to the Z.C.M.I. store and bought the prizes they had won. So you see, J.D., Papa isn't going to pay much attention to your story, but he will pay a lot of attention to mine."

I didn't like the sound of that. "What do you mean by that?" I asked.

Tom shrugged. "I will naturally have to tell Papa that you tried to blackmail me out of ten per cent of the profits," he said. "My guess is that you will lose your allowance for a month, maybe longer, and receive at least a month of the silent treatment."

Talk about being a step ahead of somebody. The Great Brain was a mile ahead of me. And I couldn't help wondering when I looked in a mirror why I didn't see the head of a donkey on my shoulders.

"Forget about making me a partner," I said. "I'm sorry I tried to blackmail you."

"I accept your apology," Tom said. "Face it, J.D., you haven't got the brains to blackmail anybody. That is why I forgive you."

I watched Tom take down the wheel of fortune.

"What are you going to do with it?" I asked.

"I've taken the fellows for all the spending money they have," Tom said, "except for Parley and Pete. I'll put the wheel of fortune up in my loft until the rest of the fellows have saved up some money."

I waited until Tom came down from the loft and helped him put the prizes in a cardboard box. Then Tom put his arm around my shoulders.

"How much did you lose, J.D.?" he asked sympathetically.

"Twenty-five cents this morning," I said, "and fifteen cents this afternoon."

"I would gladly give you back your forty cents," Tom said, "except for one thing."

I couldn't think of any possible reason why he would gladly give me my money back.

"What's that?" I asked.

"I want this experience to teach you never to gamble again," Tom said. "I'm doing it for your own good."

Maybe it was for my own good. But for my money it would have done me a lot more good to get back my forty cents, although I must admit it taught me never to gamble again.

CHAPTER EIGHT

The Game of Outlaw and Posse

ALTHOUGH I'D BEEN FOOL enough to play it, for my money the wheel of fortune was an out and out swindle. Only two fellows had won money and about twenty-five kids had lost money, including me. I guess the fellows who lost were too ashamed to admit they had been swindled or too dumb to know it. They continued to talk to Tom and play with him. But I did notice they all stopped making fun of his great brain. And the fortune Tom made must have satisfied his money-loving heart at least for a little while. He didn't even make a bet until a couple of weeks later.

The bet was made on a Friday afternoon. We had been playing scrub football on Smith's vacant lot after school let out. We stopped when it was time to go home and do the evening chores, but as usual on Fridays, we talked about what we were going to do the next day before going home. Seth Smith was the first one to make a suggestion.

"How about playing outlaw and posse tomorrow?" he asked.

Pete Kyle shook his head. "It is my turn to be the outlaw," he said, "but I can't play. Got to help Pa fix the roof on our barn."

Parley pushed his coonskin cap to the back of his head. "How about letting me be the outlaw in your place?" he asked.

"Sure," Pete said.

"The posse will never catch me," Parley said, as confident as a rabbit being chased by a snail.

Tom looked at him. "I'll bet we would if I was the sheriff," he said. "But it is Danny's turn to be the sheriff."

"Not me," Danny said. "I don't want to be the sheriff if Parley is going to be the outlaw. You can be the sheriff, Tom."

I didn't blame Danny for not wanting to be sheriff. The last time he'd been sheriff Parley had been the outlaw, and the posse hadn't captured him.

Parley tapped Tom on the chest with his finger. "Bet two-bits the posse doesn't capture me," he said.

"You seem mighty sure of yourself," Tom said.

"I'm as sure as sure can be," Parley said.

"Then why just a quarter?" Tom asked. "Why not bet a dollar?"

We all stared bug-eyed at Tom. A dollar was a fortune to every kid there except The Great Brain.

"You figured I'd back down if you made the bet a dollar," Parley said. "But you are forgetting I won more than a dollar on the wheel of fortune. I'm going to call your bluff. A dollar says the posse doesn't capture me."

"It's a bet," Tom said. "All of you fellows with horses who want to play the game meet in the alley in back of my place tomorrow morning after chores. And this time bring food an outlaw and posse would have. Just beef jerky and hardtack. I don't want anybody showing up with sandwiches and cookies like you did last time, Seth."

For my money Tom would have a better chance of winning a bet that our milk cow could jump over our barn. Parley had learned everything there was to know about tracking from his father. Trying to track him down would be like tracking a rabbit over a lava bed. Parley had outwitted the posse every time he'd been the outlaw. Of course Tom hadn't been the sheriff any of those times. And the sheriff was in complete charge and the deputies had to follow his orders. I was thinking about this as Tom and I walked toward home.

"I'll bet you were surprised when Parley called your bluff," I said. "You can kiss that dollar good-bye."

"I wasn't trying to bluff him out of betting," Tom said. "I just wanted to make him bet more than a quarter. I knew he could afford to bet a dollar because of the money he won on the wheel of fortune."

"I still say you can kiss that dollar good-bye," I said.

"If that is the way you feel, J.D.," Tom said. "Why don't you get down a bet of your own?"

All of my life I'd been waiting to win a bet from The Great Brain. Papa had often said if you just had the patience to wait long enough for something to happen that someday it would happen. This was my golden opportunity.

"Bet a quarter the posse doesn't catch the outlaw," I said.

"You've got yourself a bet," Tom said.

The next morning Tom, Frankie, and I finished the chores. Eddie Huddle came over to play with Frankie. Tom and I saddled up Dusty. Parley was the first to arrive, riding his pony, Blaze. Then Seth Smith, Danny Forester, Hal Evans, Frank Jensen, and Howard Kay arrived on their horses. The rest of the fellows who owned horses had to work.

Tom and I rode double on Dusty as the outlaw and posse started for Three Falls Canyon where we played the game. The canyon was located about seven miles from town. It was named for the three waterfalls in it. The Paiute Indians believed the canyon was haunted and wouldn't enter it, and I sure as heck didn't blame them. The Paiute name for the canyon meant, *place where screaming bad spirits dwell.* The walls of the canyon were all limestone and in some places almost perpendicular. Millions of years of frost, rain, and wind had carved holes in the limestone cliffs. Some of them looked like giant honeycombs, they had so many holes in them. When the wind blew in these holes it made an eerie whistling sound like the screaming of hundreds of demons. Another eerie thing was the way the coloring in the limestone cliffs changed with the light. Cliffs that looked pink, cream, and purple in the sunlight changed to vermilion, yellow, and orange when the sun went behind a cloud.

Every time I entered the canyon I wondered if some ancestor of mine could have been a Paiute Indian because I felt the same way they did about the canyon. I wouldn't have gone there alone for all the candy in the Z.C.M.I. store. In addition, bobcats, mountain lions, wolves, and even bears had been killed in the canyon by hunters and trappers. For my money it was a good place for a fellow to have a lot of company.

We arrived at the mouth of the canyon before noon. We all ate some beef jerky and hardtack and drank water from the stream that ran down the canyon. Then Tom took out the watch he had received for Christmas.

"You all know the rules," he said. "The posse gives the outlaw a fifteen minute head start. Then the posse has two hours to track down the outlaw and get close enough to touch him to arrest him, or the outlaw wins. It is now a quarter past twelve. That means the outlaw must be caught by two thirty. All right, outlaw, get going."

Parley jumped on Blaze and rode up the canyon on the trail used by hunters and trappers. Tom sat on a log holding the watch in his hand until the fifteen minutes were up. Then he put the watch in his pocket and stood up.

"Mount up, men," he ordered. "We've got an outlaw to capture."

We rode up the canyon following the trail. The hoofprints of the outlaw's horse were easy to follow because there had been a light rain the night before. Birds began making noises in the trees. I saw crossbills, Clark's nutcrackers, and a lot of gray jays. The jays were better known as camp robbers. They were the most daring thieves of all birds. They would steal a piece of bread right out of your hand. One time on our annual fishing trip Papa had just put bacon and eggs on our tin plates when some camp robbers swooped down and stole the bacon right off our plates.

The canyon was too narrow for farming or grazing livestock. It was more of a gorge than a canyon, less than a hundred feet wide in most places, and in some places only about twenty-five feet wide. We had traveled for about fifteen minutes when Tom called a halt.

"The outlaw rode his horse at a gallop or trot this far," he said. "But now the hoofprints show he slowed his horse down to a walk. So keep a sharp eye for signs where he might have left his horse and tried to escape on foot."

We followed the trail around a bend in the canyon. Parley's pony, Blaze, was standing by himself eating some grass by the trail. Tom dismounted. He walked all round the pony looking for footprints or bent grass caused by footsteps but couldn't find any. He led Blaze over to me and handed me the reins.

"You ride the outlaw's horse," he said. Then he went over and sat down on a log. He sat there so long Danny finally rode over beside him.

"Are you giving up already, Sheriff?" he asked.

"No," Tom said as he stood up. "We know the outlaw left his horse but he didn't get off on the ground or we would have seen signs of footprints along the trail."

"Maybe he erased his footprints with a bush," Danny said.

"The ground is too wet for that," Tom said.

"But there is no other way to get off a horse," Danny protested.

"Yes, there is," Tom said. "We will have to backtrack."

Tom mounted Dusty and we started back the way we had come. But this time Tom wasn't looking at the trail. He was looking up at trees. When we reached the place where the outlaw had walked his horse Tom called a halt. He pointed at a big limb of an aspen tree that hung about twelve feet above the trail.

"See how the small branches on that big limb are broken," he said. "That is how the outlaw left his horse."

We all stared at the limb. Danny put into words what we were all thinking.

"Impossible," he said. "The outlaw couldn't reach it from his saddle."

"You are forgetting," Tom said, "that we are dealing with an outlaw who won prizes for trick riding at county fairs before he became an outlaw. This is where he walked his horse. He stood up on the rump of the horse and grabbed the limb as they got under it. Then he hoisted himself up on the limb after giving his horse a command to keep going. See how the small branches are broken all the way to the trunk of the tree. Dismount, men."

We got off our horses and walked to the trunk of the big tree. Tom pointed at another big limb going in the opposite direction.

"See the small broken branches on that one," he said. "The outlaw used it so he could drop more than twenty feet away from the trail."

Sure enough we found footprints where the outlaw had dropped to the ground from the limb.

"We will have to track him on foot," Tom said. "Deputies Evans, Jensen, and Kay take the horses along the trail and meet us at the first waterfall. The rest of you men come with me."

I guess the outlaw figured he had outwitted the posse with that tree trick. He made no attempt to avoid leaving footprints or bent grass caused by footsteps all the way to the first waterfall. There the footprints disappeared. Floods roaring down the canyon over the centuries had washed away all dirt and grass around the waterfall leaving just rocks and big boulders right up to the canyon walls. The outlaw must have washed off his boots because there wasn't a sign of any mud or grass from the soles of his boots on the rocks or boulders.

"Stake the horses," Tom ordered. "Deputies Forester and Smith go above the waterfall on the left side and look for signs of footprints showing the outlaw went farther up the canyon. The rest of you deputies take the other side."

I started to follow orders but Tom grabbed my arm.

"Wait here with me," he said.

Then Tom waited until the deputies were out of earshot. "I just sent them up there so they couldn't hear," he said. "Now, I'll tell you why I bet Parley a dollar. This is where the outlaw's trail disappeared every time Parley was the outlaw. My great brain figured out how he outwitted the posse. He removed his clothes and hid them under rocks or bushes."

"Why would he do that?" I asked.

"So he could go in under the waterfall and hide there until the posse went farther up the canyon," Tom said. "Then he came out, got dressed, and went back to the mouth of the canyon where he waited until the posse returned after the two hours were up. Now take off your clothes and go under the waterfall and arrest that outlaw."

"Why me?" I asked, seeing as how it was going to cost me a quarter if Parley was there.

"Because you are just a deputy," Tom said, "and I am a sheriff giving you an order."

I stripped naked and waded in under the waterfall. There was room to hide there all right, under an overhanging ledge of rock, but no outlaw. The deputies had returned when I came out shivering from the cold water. Tom had told them what I was doing. It was almost worth the trip in under the waterfall to see the look of disappointment on The Great Brain's face when I told him there was no outlaw there.

"Then he must have gone farther up the canyon," Tom said.

"But," Danny protested, "we didn't see any signs of footprints above the waterfall."

"He walked on rocks to the stream," Tom said, "and then waded upstream. The rules say the outlaw can't go any farther than the second waterfall, and I'll bet we find him hiding under it. But just to make sure, deputies Forester and Smith take the left side of the stream and look for footprints where the outlaw might have left it. The rest of you come with me." Then Tom turned to me. "Can't wait for you to get dry and dressed. You wait here."

I sat on a big boulder to let the sun dry me as the posse left. The last thing I wanted was to be left alone in the canyon. The eerie whistling of the wind in the honeycombed cliffs was enough to make me start seeing imaginary demons. I knew bobcats, mountain lions, wolves, and bears wouldn't attack a man on a horse or a group of men. But one little kid sitting naked on a boulder might look like a nice tasty morsel to them.

I ran to where the horses were staked and got on Dusty. The posse was out of earshot by this time or I would have hollered for help even if it did make me a fraidy-cat. I sat on Dusty listening to the whistling of the wind and staring up at the limestone cliffs. I decided to heck with it, I'd get dressed without waiting to dry off, and run to catch up with the posse. But just then I saw fur moving on a ledge about twenty feet from the floor of the canyon. I wondered how in the world an animal got up on that ledge. Then Parley peeked over the edge and I knew it had been his coonskin cap that I had seen. He had climbed up to the ledge using the holes in the cliff for handholds and toeholds, and then lain down flat so we couldn't see him. No wonder the posse had never caught him.

I jumped off Dusty. "I captured you!" I shouted. "Come on down!"

Parley stared down at me. "I thought you had all gone up the canyon," he shouted.

"You thought wrong!" I shouted right back.

"I'm not captured until the sheriff or a deputy gets near enough to touch me," he called.

I got dressed in nothing flat with Parley watching me. I knew he thought I'd go after the posse and he could climb down and escape while I was doing it. Well I had a surprise for him. Maybe the canyon did frighten me, but I wasn't afraid to climb up to that ledge.

I walked to the cliff and looked up at him. "If you don't come down," I shouted, "I'm coming up."

"Come ahead," Parley yelled and I knew from the way he was looking down at me that he thought I was afraid to try it.

I got a handhold and toehold and started climbing up the cliff. Parley watched me until I'd climbed about halfway to the ledge.

"You'll have to climb higher than this ledge to capture me!" he shouted.

And I'll be an eagle that flies backward if he didn't start climbing straight up the cliff. I climbed back to the bottom of the canyon. It was about seventy-five feet from the ledge to the top of the cliff.

"Come back you fool!" I screamed at him. "You'll fall and be killed!"

But Parley kept right on climbing up the side of the cliff using holes for handholds and toeholds. I was so fascinated with awe and terror that I just stood there watching him. He was about halfway to the top when the toehold he was using with his right foot broke loose from the cliff and a big chunk of limestone came tumbling down. Parley hunted around with the toe of his right foot trying to find another hole. But there wasn't any he could reach. He couldn't go up without a toehold. He couldn't come down because the piece of limestone that had broken off was a handhold he had used going up. I knew that if he let go and fell on the rocks and boulders below he would be killed.

"Help!" Parley screamed as he realized he was trapped.

"Hang on!" I shouted. "I'll get help!"

I scrambled over the boulders to the top of the waterfall. Then I began running along the bank of the stream screaming for help. I knew I could catch up with the posse if I could just keep on running. My breath felt like flames of fire in my throat. My legs began to tremble so much I thought I'd fall down. Then I remembered something Papa had said one time. He had said all human beings develop superhuman strength when faced with great danger. Papa was right. The thought seemed to give me the strength to keep going. And finally I saw the posse.

"Help!" I shouted. "Help! Help!"

They all turned around and came running toward me. Tom reached me first.

"What's the matter, J. D.?" he asked.

"Parley's on the cliff by the waterfall!" I said. "He can't go up and he can't come down!"

I had a hard time keeping up with the others as we ran back to the waterfall. Parley was still hanging on the cliff screaming for help.

"Hang on, Parley!" Tom shouted. "We'll rescue you!"

Then he looked at the cliff for a couple of seconds. "Danny," he said, "you and Seth ride back to the mouth of the canyon and come back on top. When you get there tie your lariats together. Then tie one end to the pommel of the saddle on your horse, Danny. Seth, you let the lariat down over the cliff so Danny can use his horse to pull up Parley and me."

Danny pointed at Tom. "Parley and you?" he asked.

"It will take you about an hour to get to the top," Tom said. "Maybe Parley can't hold on that long. I'll scale the cliff taking two lariats with me. I'll tie one end to a tree and let myself down the cliff so I can hold Parley until you get there. All right, get going."

Danny and Seth ran toward their horses with Tom and the rest of us following. They mounted and rode down the canyon. Tom removed the lariats from Dusty and Blaze. He tied them together. Then he coiled them and slipped the coil over his head on his left shoulder and under his right arm. I looked up at the cliff which was about a hundred feet high and became very frightened.

"Please don't try it," I pleaded. "What happened to Parley might happen to you. Please don't take the chance."

"I'd take a chance of climbing that cliff any day in the week," Tom said, "to save Parley's life and make a dollar." He handed me his watch. "Look at the time when I reach Parley."

Then he ran toward the cliff shouting, "Hang on, Parley, I'm coming!"

Hal Evans, Frank Jensen, Howard Kay, and I stood watching as Tom began climbing the cliff. When he reached the ledge he studied the side of the cliff for a couple of seconds. Then he walked along the ledge and started climbing up the face of the cliff about fifteen feet from where Parley had been climbing. But Tom was climbing different than Parley had. He was sort of zigzagging up the cliff. He would climb several feet and then study the cliff above him. Sometimes he went to the right and sometimes to the left before continuing straight up. I knew he was doing this to pick the best holes in the cliff to use as handholds and toeholds. We could hear him shouting encouragement to Parley. We groaned with relief each time Tom got another handhold or toehold. When he was opposite Parley he stopped.

"Just hang on!" he shouted.

"Hurry, Tom, please!" Parley yelled. "My hands are going numb! I can't hold on much longer!"

"I'll get you out of this!" Tom shouted. "Just hang on!"

Up, up, up the face of the honeycombed cliff Tom climbed until at last he reached the rim where the canyon wall sloped toward the top. There were scraggly cedar and pine trees growing between cracks in rocks. Tom took hold of a cedar tree and tested it. Then he used the tree to pull himself up over the rim of the cliff.

"He did it!" I heard Hal yell.

Then he, Frank, and Howard began shouting and jumping up and down. But I was so stunned with relief that I couldn't speak or move. I watched Tom use scraggly cedar and pine trees and rocks to climb to the top of the canyon. Then he disappeared. I knew he was tying one end of the double lariat to a big tree on top. I don't believe I blinked my eyes until I saw him again.

Tom came down the sloping part of the canyon wall using the lariat to hold himself and uncoiling it as he went. He stopped at the rim of the cliff and tossed the coiled-up part of the double lariat over the edge. When it uncoiled it was about six feet from Parley. I knew why Tom didn't put the lariat any closer to Parley. He was afraid Parley might try to grab it with one hand and wouldn't be able to hold himself with just one handhold. I watched with mixed feelings of pride and awe as Tom let himself down the face of the cliff hand over hand on the lariat.

"Hang on for just a couple more seconds!" he shouted when he got opposite Parley.

Then he held his weight with his left hand while he made a noose round his body under the armpits with his right hand. He tightened the noose and then tested it. Then he pushed himself away from the cliff with his feet until he was standing practically horizontal to the cliff with the double lariat holding his weight. He walked sideways like that until he was straddling Parley's body. Then he bent his legs until his knees were straddling Parley's legs. I watched him put his arms around Parley's chest. Then he must have told Parley to let go of the handholds. I don't know if it was the wind or what, but they both began to spin slowly around in the air.

I didn't realize until that moment that my left hand was hurting. I looked at it. I'd been squeezing Tom's pocket watch so hard the case had made a deep impression in my palm. I opened the lid of the case and looked at the time.

Howard touched my arm. "What time is it." he asked.

I showed him the watch. "Ten minutes past two," I said.

"How long have Seth and Danny been gone?" he asked.

"I don't know," I answered.

Hal and Frank were near enough to hear.

"I figure they've been gone almost half an hour," Hal said. "That means Tom will have to hold Parley for almost half an hour."

"Look," Frank said pointing up. "Parley can't help to hold himself because he'd have to raise his arms in back of his head. That would make it harder for Tom to hold him. That's why Tom is taking a leg scissor hold too."

I saw Tom had wrapped his legs around Parley's legs and taken a scissor hold by locking his ankles. This would help him support Parley's weight.

I don't know how long it was before Danny and Seth reached the top. I only know that I felt as though I'd aged ten years before I finally saw Seth. He and Danny had followed Tom's instructions. Seth came down the slope of the canyon holding himself by the double lariat tied to the pommel of Danny's saddle on Danny's horse. I couldn't see Danny or the horse. When Seth got to the rim of the cliff he looked over the edge and tossed the coiled-up part of the lariat over the side. When it uncoiled I could see there was a noose on the end of it.

Seth shouted something at Tom and Parley. I couldn't hear what it was because the wind was blowing stronger, making a loud whistling noise in the honeycombed cliff. But I could see what was happening. The wind was blowing the lariat out of Parley's reach. Seth moved to the left with the lariat. Then the wind blew the noose part so Parley could grab it.

I watched Parley get the noose over his head and under his armpits while Tom held him. He lost his coonskin cap doing this and it fell to the canyon floor. Then after tightening the noose Parley waved at Seth. Seth took up the slack in the lariat and went to the top of the canyon. A moment later I saw Parley being slowly lifted to the rim of the cliff by Danny's horse. When Parley reached the slope he tried to stand up but his legs gave out under him. He let himself be dragged all the way to the top.

Hal, Frank, and Howard began to cheer and shout and jump up and down. I didn't join them. I was thinking only of Tom. It seemed like a long time before Seth came back to the rim of the cliff and tossed the coiled-up lariat over the edge. Tom grabbed the noose part. He had a little trouble getting it under his armpits on account of the other lariat, but he finally made it. He tightened the noose.

"Haul away!" he shouted as he waved at Seth.

Not until my brother was safe on top did I join Hal, Frank, and Howard in cheering and jumping up and down with joy. Then we rode to the mouth of the canyon with me riding Dusty and leading Blaze. We arrived a few minutes before Tom and the others got there riding double on Seth's and Danny's horses. Parley looked a little pale but he sure didn't act like a fellow who has just faced death.

"Where's my coonskin cap?" he asked.

"Boy, oh, boy," I said with disgust, "if that doesn't take the cake. Tom just saved your life, and all you're worrying about is your old coonskin cap."

"I thanked Tom for saving my life," he said. "Now where is it?"

"At the bottom of the cliff where it fell," I answered.

And I'll be a rooster that lays eggs if Parley didn't jump on Blaze and ride up the canyon to get his precious coonskin cap.

Danny watched Parley ride away and then looked at Tom. "Parley would be dead instead of worrying about his coonskin cap if it weren't for you," he said. "He told Seth and me when we got him on top that you reached him just in time. He said he couldn't have held on for more than a few minutes longer."

We sat on logs talking about the rescue until Parley returned wearing his coonskin cap. He jumped off Blaze.

Tom stood up. "We've got two things to settle before we start back," he said. "First, we can't tell anybody what happened today."

"Why not?" I asked. "You are a hero and everybody should know it."

"That would include our parents," Tom said. "And the parents of every kid in town. And you know what that would mean. They would never let any of their sons come here to play outlaw and posse again, including us."

We all agreed Tom was right and took an oath never to tell.

Parley pushed his coonskin cap to the back of his head. "Now, that is settled," he said. "What was the other thing?"

Tom looked at me. "J.D., what time was it when I reached Parley on the cliff?" he asked.

"I looked at the watch like you said," I told him. "It was ten minutes past two and Howard is my witness."

Tom then turned to Parley. "The deadline for the posse to catch you was two thirty," he said. "That means you lost the bet and owe me a dollar."

"I didn't bring a dollar with me," Parley said, "because I was sure the posse wouldn't catch me. I used that ledge to outwit the posse the other times I was the outlaw and thought I could do it again. I just lay there until the posse went farther up the canyon and then climbed down and came back here."

"We go right by your place on the way home," Tom said. "You can give me the dollar then."

When we got to the Benson home Parley went into the house. He came out and handed Tom a silver dollar. Tom and I rode Dusty to our barn. We unsaddled the mustang and gave him a rubdown. It was time to start doing the evening chores when we came out of the barn.

"Know something, J.D.?" Tom said as he took the silver dollar from his pocket and began flipping it up and down in his hand. "This is a very important dollar."

"Why shouldn't it be?" I asked. "It is the first honest dollar you ever earned in your life."

"I did work very hard for this dollar," Tom said. "I think I'll have it framed."

I knew why he wanted to frame the dollar. It wasn't to remind him that he'd saved Parley's life. It was so when people said The Great Brain had never earned an honest dollar in his life, Tom could show it to them and prove they were wrong.

"Speaking of money," Tom said as we reached the corral gate, "before we start doing the chores let's go up to your room so you can pay me the quarter you owe me."

"Boy, oh, boy," I said, "you've got a lot of nerve asking me for that quarter we bet. If it hadn't been for me the posse would never have captured the outlaw, and you would have lost a dollar to Parley and a quarter to me."

"But the posse did capture the outlaw," Tom said, "which means you owe me twenty-five cents. The trouble with you, J.D., is that you don't play to win. You could have won the bet very easily."

"And just how do you figure that?" I asked.

"If I'd been in your shoes," Tom said, "I would have pretended I hadn't seen Parley on the ledge. Then I would have gotten dressed and followed the posse upstream, giving Parley the chance to outwit the posse."

"But that would be cheating the sheriff and the deputies," I protested.

"It was only a game," Tom said. "And when you play any game play it to win and don't worry about the other fellow."

I knew right then life was just a game of outwitting the other fellow to The Great Brain. He wouldn't reform until cows started laying eggs and chickens began having calves. I admit Tom did use his great brain to do good things like solving the train robbery and murder, giving kids a chance to see their first magic show, and saving Parley's life. But his money-loving heart made him do bad things like swindling the fellows by betting he could ride Chalky and cheating them with his wheel of fortune.

Maybe the good he did with his great brain outweighed the bad he did with his money-loving heart. And maybe not. I don't know. But one thing I did know for sure was that someday Tom would make the name of Fitzgerald famous. His great brain would make him the savior of his country or his money-loving heart make him the master confidence man of all time. And some day for sure our family would either be visiting Tom in the White House or in prison.